T0131780

Keeping In Line

Keeping It Live

Keeping In Line

Courtney Brandt

iUniverse, Inc.
New York Bloomington

iUniverse books may be ordered through booksellers or by contacting:

iUniverse
1663 Liberty Drive
Bloomington, IN 47403
www.iuniverse.com
1-800-Authors (1-800-288-4677)

Because of the dynamic nature of the Internet, any Web addresses or links contained in this book may have changed since publication and may no longer be valid. The views expressed in this work are solely those of the author and do not necessarily reflect the views of the publisher, and the publisher hereby disclaims any responsibility for them.

ISBN: 978-1-4401-8208-2 (sc)
ISBN: 978-1-4401-8209-9 (ebook)

Printed in the United States of America

iUniverse rev. date: 11/09/09

Dedicated to B and Rae…

and the many fun times we've had around the world.

Room 631.

Always crowded.

Always open.

Double doors into a new world.

The best Coke machine in the school.

The best "toys,"

Nearly the size of a closet.

Barely enough room to function, but we make do.

The best groups come out of this room.

The most dedicated and motivated.

Nothing can compare to the things this room can do.

We don't need nice tv sets, video gaming systems or couches.

We have our instruments.

These walls have absorbed the sounds of thousands of kids.

The music stands have held hours of music.

This room will feel empty without me.

But it will soon be full of new kids, starting their adventures in room 631.

*- by **Krissi Banks** (used with permission)*

Contents

Prologue: Can I Graduate?

Dear Journal,

I can't believe Lucy's class has graduated. It seems like only yesterday I was meeting all of them for the first time as a little naïve freshman. Not that much has changed on that front...but I'm getting ahead of myself. Where are my manners? As I'm starting a new journal, I'd better reintroduce myself although nothing really exciting or revolutionary has changed in the four days since I ended my last journal and began this one. My name is Bronwyn Margaret Flueger. I am a (recently turned) fifteen year old and officially (school got out today) in between the summer of my freshman and sophomore year, so I'm not sure if that makes me froshmore or a sophoman. Of course, there's one thing that pretty much sets me apart from most girls my age:

I'm a drummer.

So, how would I describe myself? (Or, more honestly, how do I want to remember myself when I look back and read this one day?) Well, I'm on the short side of 5'2" with red hair. I wish it was a prettier red, because in reality it's kind of a warm scarlet color that clashes with everything. It is my own natural color which is cool, but it is a wild curly mess and some days I'd rather I didn't have any hair at all. My eyes are a blueish gray and I struggle to fill a B cup.

Introductory sidebar over, what's the big deal about graduation? Firstly, I had to go and see my friends on their big night. The seniors of the Forrest Hills drum line are some pretty important people to this froshmore/sophoman. They were all members of a group that is pretty much my reason for living – the drum line.

And I'll go ahead and brag here because I am marching SNARE this season! Every time I write it or read it or hear other people talk about it, I still can't believe it's actually real. I keep expecting to wake up, get a call from Henry (our Instructor) and have him tell me it's all some huge mistake and I'm actually lucky to be playing the triangle. This is something Lucy (more on her later) tells me I need to work on. Generally, percussionists are gifted with a healthy dose of attitude and confidence. As you might be able to guess, I missed that class. I know I'm good; I just sometimes have problems projecting that image. Not helping the scenario are some very intense upperclassmen that make up the rest of my section. On paper, I know I can keep up with them, but reality is a different matter. I'm going to have to be my best this year because I know everyone's going to be watching and waiting for me to mess up. I was the only freshman to make the jump to the snare line and of course, there's the whole "only" girl thing to go with it. I'm the first girl in five generations of the Forrest Hills Line to make snare. There's a lot of pressure, but I'm not going to let it get to me. Fortunately, I do get a bit of time to build myself up to a place where I feel a comfortable and confident member of the section. We're having a number of practices – snares only – during the summer. That should give me enough time to figure out that I actually belong with them.

Okay, okay…so, back to graduation. Remember those seniors I was mentioning? There was one very important person among them – Lucy Karate. So, who is Lucy and why is she my hero? Well, you'd have to consult journals 7-9 for those stories, but I'll give you the short version she's basically everything a drum line girl could hope to be except maybe Captain, which is totally what I want to be thanks to Lucy. Remember that naïve little freshman I was telling you about? Well, I would be even more socially awkward had it not been for Lucy. She took me under her wing last season and literally transformed me into a different person. Without getting all Lifetime Original story, I can assure you that when I started at Forrest Hills, I was this shy dork who didn't know how to flirt, let alone talk to boys my age (kind of a problem considering my chosen section). Now, I will admit I still have a long way to go, but I have a lot more confidence on that front. I fully believe the confidence Lucy gave me allowed me to 'man up' and have the proverbial cajones to audition for (and make) snare.

In addition to Lucy, I'm also very sad to see Tom go. I'll admit, next to my weird infatuation on Drew (more on that later), I had a bit of a crush on the former quint section leader…but watching him with Jewel, well, it's not like he and I were ever going to be anything, so he should be happy with someone. He always made me laugh and paid attention to me, which, when you're a freshman is sometimes the best you're going to get.

I'm definitely going to miss them, but with all the ways to keep in touch these days, I know they won't be too far away. Don't ask me why, but I have a feeling I'll need Lucy in my life if I'm going to make it through this season alive. Fortunately, she's going to State which isn't that far and she promised to try and come back for a game or two.

Well, I'd better go and practice. In fact, I'm surprised J.D. hasn't already called me to see if I'm drumming. As I'm sure I've mentioned in previous journals, J.D. is going to be a senior and was recently chosen as this year's captain. Oh, I mean Captain with a capital C. And actually, if I wrote his name like all the Guard girls say it I would be writing Jay Deeeeeeeeeeee while going all googly eyed. Now, I'll admit he is cute, but Lucy warned me to stay away from dating in the Line, making my life 'unnecessarily complicated.' It's no big deal for me – when I'm with the rest of the Line after summer, I'm planning on concentrating on the music and drill only. Plus, I've got my eye on someone else.

Yes, even though I was very slow to admit it – I have major feelings for one of our three drum majors. His name is Drew O'Malley. He's a senior and last year when I was in Pit, we talked a lot. Well, it's not like we had deep and meaningful conversations, but we did interact on a usual basis. Anyway, once the season ended, I didn't see him that much, which was kind of sad. Furthermore, he's going to be all kinds of busy this season, so it's not like he would even have time to see me. He's the senior drum major, plus, this year Mr. Izzo decided to add an additional person to help lead the band. This is a first for us, so we'll have to see how it all works out.

I guess I'll just have to crush from across the field. Or, maybe this is the year things are different…

Oh, one more thing, back to what else? Drum line. Even though Lucy and my old section leader Molly are graduating, it's not like I'm the singular "girl" on the Line. Beth and Valerie are girls in Pit and are both freshmen this year. I met them at the Warm-up Week we had for all the incoming 8th graders. They seem cool enough, but that means, like Lucy was last year, I am the only girl on the Battery. I'm cool with it. I just hope I can get to the point Lucy was at. Everyone respected her, but they also totally knew she was a girl too. I wonder how she did that.

More later,
B

Chapter One

Summertime and the Livin's...

From beneath her stylish tan straw fedora (a congratulations-you-made-the-snare-line gift from one Lucy Karate who wanted to protect her friend's fair skin), Bronwyn Flueger lifted her cat eye tortoiseshell frames and wiped the sweat from her face. It was nearing the end of July and she was outside, drumming. Her Captain, J.D. Strauss, was either too macho or too insane to go inside or consider moving his section into the shade, so the entire snare line was sweating through their last chop busting session of the summer. Were any other members of the band practicing this early in the season? The youngest snare drummer seriously doubted it. At least the guys were lucky – they could take off their shirts. Bronwyn, however, was not yet at the comfort level where she was going to take off her shirt in front of a bunch of upperclassmen. Her own tan lines were tank top specific and she was quite comfortable with that fact.

Zoning out of the endless rudiment exercise, the sophomore focused on happier thoughts. As much as she loved drumming, pre-band camp was the following week and she couldn't wait. Bronwyn would be glad to see *anyone* besides another snare drummer. While she had earned the basic respect of the guys she had spent long hours under the sun with, she still didn't hang out with them socially. Although Bronwyn wouldn't admit it to the jealous members of her class who wanted a place in the section, J.D. had kind of beaten the fun out of being a snare drummer.

Bronwyn hadn't known what exactly to expect for her summer practices, but remembering her season last year, she certainly expected more inside jokes. More laughing. More inappropriateness. More...everything. Instead, it had been drumming, plain and simple. No friendships, no laughing, no inclusion of any kind. There were moments of fun now and then, but Bronwyn was worried about what would happen when they joined the rest of the drum line. She needed to be a part of something, needed the acceptance of the upperclassman to help her face her tormentors in the sophomore class.

1

She knew the unspoken rule – it was fine to be a girl…as long as you didn't take someone else's slot on the Line. There was one guy in particular who Bronwyn wasn't looking forward to seeing again. Tony Clarke. Tony was completely bitter Bronwyn had made the snare line and had no problem sharing his feelings with any one who would listen. She knew the underlying reason he was so upset – the earlier you are picked to be on the snare line, the better shot you have of being Captain in your senior year. It was no secret that Tony wanted to be Captain, and had considered it his birthright since they had all picked up sticks in middle school. He was irritating, but also smart enough to limit his bullying to when the section leaders weren't around.

Forcing herself to think about more positive subjects, Bronwyn looked around at the rest of the snares while they finished the exercise. There was tall Lance, a senior who had marched snare last season and two years on bass before that. Since she had had her own issues to worry about, Bronwyn hadn't got caught up in the politics of the fierce battle for the drum line Captain title. Lance, a veteran with three years on the Line was livid that J.D., who had transferred to Forrest Hills only last season, was named Captain instead of him. The seniors had worked out some of their differences over the summer, but Bronwyn knew there was still some unresolved tension between them. Lance was always the first to comment if J.D. did something wrong, the first to come up with an alternative way to do something, and the first to point out if any of the other snares weren't doing their best. Almost everyone on the Line thought J.D. would do a good job, except for Lance's loyal friends, Mark (now on quints) and Jared (the bass Lieutenant) who were also unhappy with the selection of J.D. as Captain. Bronwyn decided it was probably in her best interest to stay under the radar, which had been easy so far, as she didn't march next to either Lance or J.D.

With six snares in total, Lance and J.D. were in the middle with Adam and Bronwyn on one end (dubbing themselves the West Side) and Kevin and Scott on the other end (representing the East Side). Adam was the sanest person on the snare line to march next to, and she felt grateful for her placement.

Holding his stick up, J.D. signaled for the end of the exercise. The snares smartly tucked their sticks away. For whatever reason, J.D. was in a bad mood, which meant they had to be at attention and on top of their game or risk doing countless push-ups. In the absence of Henry, who was touring during the summer as a caption head with DCI, J.D. was the law. As Bronwyn gritted her teeth, aching to relax her shoulders, she maintained her fixed stance. They had been fortunate their Captain had been in a good mood at the start of practice and allowed them to practice on their stands, rather than use their carriers. As a particularly annoying bead of sweat dripped down her back, she struggled to maintain her composure. They couldn't break attention until J.D. released them, which was at least one thing Lance and J.D. agreed on.

J.D. finally said, "Okay, we're done for today. I'm going on vacation tomorrow, so the next time I see all of you will be at band camp."

Adam made a motion to leave.

"Did I tell you to break attention?"

Adam frowned, "No."

"Twenty ought to do it."

Adam balanced his wrapped sticks on his snare drum and began doing push-ups. Bronwyn had to control herself from staring at his defined back and shoulder muscles. J.D. continued talking, "When we get to band camp I expect the concentration we had at these practices will remain. We are the most talented section in the drum line and have to set an example for the rest of the Battery. You're free to go."

Bronwyn secretly suspected a lot of J.D.'s insane militaristic tendencies were due to his past. Before joining the Forrest Hills Drum Line (and the high school that went with it), he had attended military school and marched a summer with Drum Corps International (among band geeks, more commonly known as DCI). He had taken off from the Corps this summer to concentrate on being Captain and applying for college. Still, it was J.D.'s way or the highway and Bronwyn was too young and inexperienced on the Battery to question anyone's leadership styles.

Pre-band camp finally arrived. Bronwyn said goodbye to her dad as they pulled into the high school's familiar parking lot. She couldn't wait for the day she was able to drive herself to school. Although she knew Ben, a junior in the tenor section, lived close to her house, Bronwyn hadn't quite built up the confidence to ask him for a ride just yet.

"Have a good practice, honey!"

"I'll call you when I need to be picked up," Bronwyn answered as she slung her snare over one shoulder and walked towards the school. Usually not overly concerned with her appearance, the redhead had put a lot of consideration into what she was wearing today. She wanted to define herself and move away from the shy, naïve persona she had been known for during her ninth grade year. Over the summer, she had searched thrift stores until she found the perfect T-shirt (emblazoned with "Arizona is for Lovers" across a faded yellow background) and paired it with olive colored corduroy shorts to wear for her first official practice. She had observed how the other snares dressed and wanted to look, at least on the surface, like she belonged. Interestingly enough, her Captain was the one who looked like he didn't belong. J.D. was preppy with a capital P and Bronwyn wasn't about to be caught dead in pressed khaki shorts and a polo shirt with the collar flipped up. The redhead knew everyone on the Battery wore Oakley (or Oakley inspired) sunglasses, but decided to put her own spin on things and stuck with her retro shades. The final and most obvious difference from her shyer ninth grade self, was her new walk. Maybe it was the months of wearing the drum, but somehow, she had finally developed a walk that had attitude.

As she approached the school, she caught the whispers that trailed in her wake. "Who is *she*?"

"Is that a snare she's carrying?"

"Who let her carry their drum?"

Bronwyn was amazed at how quickly everyone had forgotten her Battery designation. She turned a corner to find Tony and the rest of the sophomore drummers. She had almost passed the group when her arch nemesis snidely called out, "I still think they mixed up the results of our auditions, Flueger."

Bronwyn looked straight ahead. She and Stewie (late one night over the summer she had decided that her drum had a name, and that name was Stewie) kept walking, choosing not to acknowledge the insult.

Angered by her lack of response, Tony called after her, "You might as well just put down the drum now before Henry or J.D. has to publicly embarrass you by removing you from the Line."

Bronwyn was about to respond when Drew unexpectedly came to her rescue. As a member of the Pit, Bronwyn had a bit of an unorthodox relationship with the drum major from the previous season. As much as her daydreams said otherwise, she would classify them as 'friendly,' but not 'friends.'

Drew replied on her behalf, "From what I hear, Bronwyn is kicking ass and taking names."

While blushing slightly, Bronwyn stuck out her tongue from behind Drew and followed him into the band room. She watched the blonde senior approach some of the Brass players and desperately wished she had said 'thank you', or something flirty, instead of doing or saying absolutely nothing. Still grumbling to herself, she left Stewie in the percussion room and sat down next to her best friends: Meredith (a sax player) and Megan (a flautist) and high-fived the rest of her band friends, Tyler (a Sousaphone) and Pete (a trumpet).

Bronwyn asked, "What did I miss?"

Meredith answered, "We're discussing which bus we're going to sign up for this season."

"I think I have to sign up for the drum line bus," Bronwyn replied glumly, not wanting to admit how nervous she was to have to ride the percussion bus. The sophomore snare remembered the previous season when the Line was headed to one of the Indoor competitions. Lucy was sitting with Tom and

Bronwyn was sitting by herself in the front of the bus. It seemed everyone else had easily found a seat mate, leaving the redhead (again) on her own.

Would this season be any different?

It was a silly question, but she wasn't sure where she would fit in. She didn't have a 'Tom' in her life like Lucy did, and she knew a lot the members of the Line would have their girlfriends on the bus anyway. Bronwyn looked across the room at Drew and wondered what bus he was going to be on.

Megan said, "Bummer."

Bronwyn agreed, "I know. J.D. is running a really tight ship this year and I don't want to risk anything, you know?"

At the name J.D., both Meredith and Megan's eyes glazed over. Bronwyn rolled her eyes, "You guys, I keep telling you – he's not that cool."

Meredith smiled broadly and replied, "Tell me the part again how you practiced with the guys and they took their shirts off..."

Sensing the topic of conversation was heading in a direction she didn't want to elaborate on, Bronwyn stood up, intent on heading to warm ups. She commented, "Ab City. I'm sure you'll all get a glimpse at band camp. I swear, any excuse they have – those shirts come off. If you find carrier tans sexy, then you're in luck. See you girls later!"

Bronwyn walked over to the percussion room where she saw Beth and Valerie standing awkwardly. The redhead remembered a year ago almost exactly to the day, when she had shown up to her first band practice. Lucy had immediately and without question taken the freshman under her wing. Bronwyn had vowed to be a cool drum line girl and attempt to do what Lucy had done for her. She forced a happy tone and asked, "Hey gals – how was your summer?"

They both mumbled generic answers.

Taking a deep breath, Bronwyn smiled and brightly said, "Do you have any questions? Us drum line girls have to stick together, after all."

At that moment Tony came in and interrupted their conversation, "Don't listen to her, girls. Bronwyn doesn't know the first thing about drum line." He then learned on one of the tall racks that held the bass drums and added flirtatiously, "If you have any questions, I'd be more than happy to show you around."

Valerie and Beth were obviously unsure of what to do, but at that moment J.D. joined everyone in the percussion room and announced, "Enough bullshitting. Everyone get their drums and get outside."

Bronwyn glared at Tony, flashed a smile at the young Pit members, grabbed a stand for her music and walked outside silently, thinking about her fellow sophomores. For whatever reason, her particular grade had produced a bumper crop of drummers who had all decided to keep playing after middle school. Tony was their ringleader and the pair had exchanged insults since their first introduction to one another. Bronwyn had quickly moved into the 'prodigy' category and Tony had not been able to get over the fact that a girl was better than he was. Worst of all, he was joined by Steve, his best friend and lackey, who was on the tenor line. Unfortunately, Bronwyn didn't have anyone like that on her side in the Line. It was a lonely existence, missing out on something everyone else seemed to have. She wasn't sure if it was because of her former shyness or maybe due to her talent as a drummer, but she had never found a close friendship in the section.

She sighed as she lined up and looked longingly across the Line, momentarily wishing she could march next to Andy, the quint Lieutenant and therefore well out of reach for Tony and his big mouth. Unfortunately, the way the Forrest Hills drum line set their arc, Bronwyn was at the end of the snares, directly next to the bass line. She *really* wasn't looking forward to an entire season of Tony, on first bass, getting in her face. She didn't want to tell J.D. about the situation because she didn't want to him to think she couldn't handle things or give her any preferential treatment. She could only hope Adam would somehow notice and maybe do something to shut Tony up.

BWAP! J.D. snapped one of his sticks down on the rim of his snare drum and got everyone's attention.

Henry, in his fifth year of instructing the Forrest Hills drummers, looked at J.D. strangely, but addressed the collected Line, "Well everyone, I hope you had a relaxing summer. I want to let you know that I'm really looking forward to the coming season. I don't have to tell you the last class left some big shoes to fill. So, I'm not going to say we're rebuilding this year, but I offer it as a challenge to you. You all know how well last year's Line did and I urge everyone to take that as a challenge to rise above. As you know, this year's half-time show is going to be something a little bit different than usual."

Bronwyn knew what he was referring to. Usually, the Forrest Hills marching band did a combination of crowd pleasing tunes. This year, Mr. Izzo had decided to do something extra. Going for a more obscure and abstract angle, the theme of the show this year was Weather. Bronwyn looked forward to what Henry would come up with, but was a bit apprehensive about how the new sound would connect with the rest of the band.

"Now, let's get warmed up. Nice and easy, Eight on a Hand."

The drummers finished the warm up and before Bronwyn knew it, practice was over. She had been so intent on looking and acting the part that she hadn't been distracted by Tony's constant antics to try and mess her up. Overall, she was proud of herself.

As they walked back to the school, J.D. came up next to her and commented, "You looked okay out there today, B."

"Th-thanks." Bronwyn knew J.D. rarely gave out anything that sounded remotely like a compliment, but that was certainly one.

Bronwyn put Stewie away in the percussion room and was on her way to call her Dad from the pay phone when Ben caught up with her, "Hey, Flueger, need a ride home?"

Bronwyn smiled appreciatively. Being an underclassman, there was nothing more embarrassing than having to wait around for your parents... especially when almost everyone else in the section could come and go whenever they wanted. She answered, "That would be great. Mind if I just call the 'rents and let them know?"

"You don't have a cell phone?"

She looked down, "Not yet – they won't let me have one until I can pay for it myself."

"Bummer – just use mine then."

"Thanks."

Bronwyn silently prayed that her sometimes overprotective, but well meaning parents, would go along with the plan. She turned away and said, "Hey Mom – I'm going to ride home with Ben tonight – he's on tenors."

The first lesson Lucy had instructed her on was how to be more forceful. Rather than ask permission, Bronwyn stated her intentions.

"Oh – okay, honey, be safe."

"Will do."

Bronwyn passed the phone back and they walked towards Ben's bright red truck.

"El Caliente," Ben said as he unlocked the door. Bronwyn got into the appropriately named ride, and it suddenly dawned on her she had never been in a car alone...with a guy. Her tongue suddenly felt huge in her mouth and she wondered how she was ever going to pull together a normal sentence.

Chapter Two

Boot Camp

Bronwyn took a deep breath and let it out slowly. Even though her brain was currently empty, she knew somewhere in her head there were some definite safe and normal topics to discuss. Then she realized Ben was looking at her, waiting for an answer.

Had he said something?

The quint player asked, "You live at the corner of Shire Way and Calley, right?"

"Yup."

Score one for me; I answered a question!

With one question successfully out of the way, Bronwyn felt braver and more confident. She scanned her head for any memories or facts she knew about Ben, other than the fact that he was a junior and he played tenors.

Bronwyn finally managed to say, "You guys sounded good today."

"Really?" His tone implied the opposite.

Bronwyn cringed, because she honestly did not know the first thing about how the quints sounded. Her attempt at small talk didn't go forward like she thought it would. She managed to reply neutrally, "Umm…yes."

"Thanks."

Many thoughts were going through Bronwyn's head, the most important of which was, *if I make a good impression, I will not have to wait for Mom and Dad to pick me up from practice every day.* Bronwyn forced herself to sound what she hoped was carefree and easy, and asked simply, "So, how was your summer?"

"It was pretty cool. I went to the beach and worked as a lifeguard for my neighborhood pool."

"Sounds like a good gig."

"It was pretty decent money – other than getting up ass early, it was alright. What did you get up to?"

As much as she wanted to badmouth her Captain and his despotic style, Bronwyn knew there was enough gossip and backtalk within the section already, so she said diplomatically, "I practiced a lot."

"Oh yeah, that's right, I forgot you're not old enough to work yet."

"Well, it's not like I'm completely without cash – I babysit sometimes. I'm hoping to start teaching after the season is over." Bronwyn was surprised at her confession. Teaching was something she had only thought about, and had never mentioned to anyone else.

"Yeah?"

"We'll see, I don't know yet."

"I bet you'd be a good teacher."

"Let's hope so – oh, here we are – it's the one with the steep driveway." As he pulled to a stop, she got out of the car, and added politely, "Thanks, Ben."

"Anytime. Take it easy."

Bronwyn closed the car door and was unsure if 'anytime' meant he would be happy to be her escort for the coming season, or he was just being polite.

To: karatechop@state.edu
From: FHHSsnaregrl@FHHS.edu

Hey Luce –

I just finished my first practice with the Battery. I think it's going to be a good season.

One problem, Tony's still being a total asshole. Any suggestions?

Have classes started for you yet? Have you moved in? Let me know!

B

To: FHHSsnaregrl@FHHS.edu
From: karatechop@state.edu

B,

Yeah, I went ahead and moved in early (with everyone's favorite pug, Pam, of course). Although I'm totally missing Wes, part of me couldn't wait to get out and on my own. I know he's doing well back in the U.K...and I should probably be missing him more, but I've been down this weird road of separation before, and it's just easier to let things go, rather than dragging them out. We'll see how it all ends up. All I can say right now is, thank goodness for Skype!

To answer your question, it won't help things if you tell Tony off publicly, because if you emasculate him in front of everyone, they will all be on his side (bros before hos, unfortunately). However, something tells me that Tony won't respond to you talking to him one on one either. So it looks like, you gotta wait him out and hope that everyone figures out what a loser he's being and calls him on it. While patience is difficult, at the end of the day, remember that you are playing snare and he is not. Either way, good luck! Vent when necessary.

Have fun at band camp! Drink lots of water!

Lucy

Bronwyn finished reading Lucy's e-mail and looked over her things as she carefully packed for the upcoming week. Last year's band camp had been one of the most fun weeks of her entire life and she was hoping this year's would be similar.

BRRRRIINNGGG!

"Shut that damn thing off!"

"Mmph. Five more minutes…"

"Sorry girls!" Bronwyn scrambled out of bed to stop the alarm clock. Much to Meredith and Megan's dismay, Bronwyn had set the speaker to extra loud because there was no way she was going to miss her first early morning warm up. Last year, as a member of the Pit, she had to sit and watch the Battery line up. This year, she was first in the makeshift equipment room and proudly put on her snare drum and walked outside into the pre-dawn air. It was tradition in the Forrest Hills marching band that they all march to breakfast together to the beats of the drum line. After Henry had warmed everyone up and the rest of the band had lined up in their respective blocks, J.D. signaled for You Know What He Did, one of everyone's favorite cadences. Because of the narrow sidewalk, the snares had to break up and march in pairs. Bronwyn fell into place at the back with Adam. They were in front of the quints, a fact Bronwyn was entirely grateful for – she knew if Tony was behind her he would probably do his best to try and trip her up.

Finally, they arrived at the dining hall. Another tradition was for the band to stand at attention until the "section of the day" was dismissed by the band director, Mr. Izzo. That section got to go in before the seniors and get first dibs on the food. From there, the dismissal went in order of classes. Bronwyn and the snares stood at perfect attention waiting directly in front of Drew, Alex, and Samantha, the drum majors. Bronwyn found it odd that

Drew had stopped near the Line. Last year, it seemed he had always been no further than five feet away from the Guard or Majorettes. As Bronwyn looked straight ahead, practicing her mean drum line face, Drew caught her eye, smiled, and winked at her. Bronwyn was so surprised by his actions that she dropped her sticks. The pieces of oak clattered loudly on the sidewalk, echoing loudly across the band standing at parade rest. J.D. looked back from the front of the Line, anger written across his face. This was not the image he wanted for his section.

Bronwyn made no move to pick up her sticks and saw Drew trying to hold back a laugh and failing miserably. Interestingly, she was less concerned about what J.D.'s punishment would be and more worried about what Drew was currently thinking. This was one of her first interactions with him in months and it wasn't exactly how she wanted to be remembered.

Mr. Izzo called the Sousas first, which didn't surprise anyone, since he used to be one himself. Then the seniors were released. J.D. carefully placed his snare down and moved into Bronwyn's space. He hissed at her, "You'll stand at attention through breakfast. Don't think I won't know if you don't."

Bronwyn blinked and was brought back to a moment during her freshman year…

Lucy was driving her home after a game near the end of the previous season. The bass drummer turned down the radio, looked seriously over at her younger passenger, and stated, "He's going to test you next year."

"Who are you talking about?"

"J.D."

Bronwyn fiddled with her bag and asked, "Seriously, why would J.D. want to test me?"

"You're going to make snare next season." It was a statement, not a question.

"Yeah right, Lucy, that's never going to happen."

"I am being completely serious. I've seen you play, you've got the chops."

"Okay, whatever."

"Well, I'm just saying, next year is going to be a totally different Line. This year is a lot of fun because we've all been together forever and everyone is cool as."

"Well, that's great," Bronwyn said sarcastically, "Are you saying next year's Line is doomed?"

"No, I'm just saying, I've seen J.D. and I know his type."

"What about Lance? You don't think he's going to lead us next year?"

"For whatever reason, I'll bet you Captain will go to J.D and you're going to have to be ready for anything he's going to dish out. He's a guy's guy and isn't going to let some girl wreck his Line."

Bronwyn looked at the passing landscape, and asked, "Do you really think I'm going to make snare?"

"Why would I lie to you? You're the future of the drum line girls at Forrest Hills. You come from a long line of some very cool chicks, you know… Anyway, I'm just saying – don't back down, don't give them excuses."

"I won't," Bronwyn promised solemnly.

Hearing people whisper loudly as they walked by her, Bronwyn was brought back to the present. She locked her blue grey eyes on J.D.'s deep brown ones, but didn't break the stare. As he and Ben walked toward the cafeteria, she overheard Ben ask, "Dude, don't you think you're being a little extreme?"

She didn't hear J.D.'s answer. She waited for the other students to be released and dreaded when it was her class's turn.

Mr. Izzo yelled out, "Sophomores!"

Bronwyn waited as everyone carefully placed their drums on the grass and soon enough Tony and Steve were right in her face. With all of the Line leadership inside, there was little she could do to stop them. Tony was the first to start, "Day one, Flueger, tsk tsk, not really a good way to start things."

Bronwyn didn't respond. Fortunately, she was at attention, which meant no talking, although internally she had a number of critical responses for Tony's meanness.

Steve nodded, while Tony continued, "Oh, that's right, you can't break attention. 'Cause if you do, I'll let J.D. know and we know how happy he'll be to hear about you messing up."

Gritting her teeth, Bronwyn took a deep breath and willed the frustrated tears from her eyes; she desperately wanted to believe all of her hard work had paid off this summer – that J.D. was fully accepting of her – that this humiliation was worth it. The reality was, although he would never admit it, she knew the senior snare didn't like having a girl in his section and this punishment was probably a weird way of him taking out some of his inner aggressions. She wondered if he would treat anyone else in the section this way.

"Take care, Flueger, we'll make sure J.D. takes his time inside."

She watched jealously as Steve and Tony went into the dining hall. As early as it was, the weather was already heating up, plus she was getting hungry. Still, there was no way she was going to break attention until J.D. personally said it was okay. When the freshmen were dismissed, Valerie and Beth gave her sympathetic looks as they walked by. Bronwyn waited and waited. Her back was cramping and she was desperate to move or stretch her legs.

How long does it take J.D. to eat his damn cereal?!

As the minutes turned into at least a half hour, Bronwyn felt as if half the band had walked by and given her strange looks before Drew passed by and asked, "Didn't you hear Izzo? You're dismissed…"

Bronwyn looked at him pleadingly, but refused to say anything. She tried to communicate the message; *you're not the one who can dismiss me…only my good for nothing Captain can do that!* She knew if she said something that would be the *exact* moment J.D. walked out and accused her of breaking attention.

"What are you doing, Drew?" A familiar voice asked.

"Trying to tell Bronwyn it's okay to break attention. You're a section leader, J.D., not a dictator. This is a public high school and not your messed up military academy."

"Well, I'm looking after *my* section, bro."

Drew stepped closer to Bronwyn, positioning himself between her and J.D., crossing his arms in front of his chest, and asked, "You know I am the senior drum major, right?"

"And?"

"That means *I* lead the band."

"Well, I'm Captain of the drum line."

With the amount of testosterone that was currently flying back and forth, Bronwyn suddenly had a mental picture of the guys unzipping their flies and measuring. She couldn't help it; the image was too random and she cracked a smile and almost burst out laughing. J.D. looked at her strangely and asked rudely, "Something funny, Flueger?"

Wisely, the sophomore snare drummer didn't answer.

J.D. looked directly at Drew and said, "You're dismissed, Flueger."

Bronwyn looked pleadingly at Drew and then walked off in the direction of the girl's dorm, rubbing her shoulders. She had definitely lost her appetite.

Chapter Three
A Simple Plan

By the time full band practice started that morning, J.D. had made sure everyone on the Line had heard about his and Drew's little standoff. Bronwyn couldn't control how much her Captain had completely blown things out of proportion, because it seemed no one wanted to hear her opinion. She also didn't understand why J.D. would want to cause trouble with the person who led the band. While occasionally there were disputes among the leadership, it was far too early in the season to have trouble like this.

"Thinks he can boss my section around..." J.D. grumbled.

Bronwyn rolled her eyes and put her snare on. After her mistake this morning, and given J.D.'s current crazy mood, she thought it would be best to keep as low a profile as possible. She was talking with some of the cymbal players when J.D. approached her.

"Flueger, if Drew ever tries to pull some shit like that again, just let me know."

Not likely, buddy, thanks to your idiocy this morning, I'm pretty sure you've made him want to avoid our section at all costs for the rest of the season. Thanks for that.

"Okay," Bronwyn said with as much sincerity as she could muster.

"Seriously, he needs to know his place here."

Bronwyn had to catch herself from rolling her eyes for the second time in as many minutes in front of J.D.

Stupid boys...why can't they just let things go?

One day blurred into the next for Bronwyn. The sophomore concentrated extra hard on making sure she was always in step and a model drummer, keeping perfect attention and not talking back. She knew J.D. was looking for any excuse to catch her messing up again and the verdict was still out for the rest of the Line. Seeing how she could easily keep up with the demands of the music, they accepted her, but there was another kind of tension present.

As Bronwyn lay awake on Thursday night, she remembered Lucy's warning from earlier in the spring...

Lucy tried to explain, "I'm not sure what it is, y'know? I don't think the guys were ever really threatened by me, because, who was I? Just some oboist who happened to become a percussionist. I wasn't interested in anything more than being on the Battery. Once I proved I could carry my weight, I guess it became a non-issue."

Bronwyn, still confused, asked, "So, you were accepted because you weren't threatening them?"

"Basically, yes. Constant flattery and stoking their egos also seems to have a positive effect."

Bronwyn smiled and asked, "So what happens if I make snare?"

Lucy thought a moment before replying, "It could be a different story. You'd probably have to do something drastic to 'prove your worth.'"

"Like what?"

"I wish I knew the answer to that, but these are teenage boys we're talking about."

Bronwyn sighed and rolled over. Even though she was physically exhausted, her mind refused to shut off and relax. Even with the steady sounds of her friends breathing around her, sleep escaped her for the moment. She wondered why the acceptance of her section was proving more difficult than she had ever thought possible. She tried to come to terms with the walking paradox she was turning into. When she was around the Line, she was quiet and reserved, but when she was on her own, away from the Line, she felt nothing but the confidence that being in the section gave her.

How do I change that?

Bronwyn was no closer to an answer the following morning. She automatically rolled out of bed and prepared for the last full day of rehearsals. Like last year, there was no break between all the events that made up band camp: sectionals, learning drill, running through the show, meals, and night activities. As much as last year had been an introduction to all things marching band, this year was definitely a glimpse at all things male. As a member of the female led Front Line last year, things hadn't been so full of testosterone.

Earlier in the week, Tony created a new game to keep himself entertained while the band was learning drill. He kept coming up with overwhelmingly gross and disgusting things to say to Bronwyn to try and get a reaction out of her. Bronwyn had taken Lucy's advice seriously and had decided it would be best just to ignore Tony. However, once in awhile the things he was saying were too gross even for Adam, and Tony would get called out for it.

Of course, Bronwyn's irritations with the first bass player were nothing compared to the clash between J.D. and Drew. The two young men were now involved in some sort of huge rivalry and the whole band was suffering because of it. Neither of them wanted to back down and neither would admit they were wrong. Worst of all, what started as a standoff between two individuals was quickly blossoming into a section wide conflict. Members of the Line weren't being obvious about it, but they were choosing to make things difficult for the drum major. If J.D. thought he was on the beat, Bronwyn only had to look up at Drew to know he was conducting something completely different. The struggle was definitely slowing the process of learning the challenging half time show.

Not that you haven't been looking up at the drum major's podium a fair amount this week…

Bronwyn wouldn't admit it to anyone, but she *had* been paying extra attention to the dreamy drum major all week from across the field. She sighed, remembering how he was usually somewhere in the vicinity of the Dance Line or Guard, chatting up its cute members. She knew things were getting a little out of control and her emotions were moving from sometime crush to borderline obsession.

It's not like he's shown you any special attention. Just because he remembered you, it doesn't mean he likes you. Also, if there was one way to piss off the Line, having something start with Drew would definitely be the way to do it…

Determined she would one day actually be accepted, and even liked among her section, Bronwyn had to admit dating Drew, or even openly liking him in the near future, had the potential to make her an outcast on her own Line.

During one of their last rehearsals on Friday afternoon, while trying to ignore Tony's antics, Bronwyn did her best to think of how to do what Lucy had suggested – to do something to 'prove herself.' Obviously, drumming her ass off wasn't going to do the trick. Suddenly, a brilliant idea occurred to her – the best way to get on the good side of the Line would be to get on the bad side of Drew.

Strangely, while she personally didn't agree with her own idea, Bronwyn could see how it might be able to solve a few of the problems she was having. If *she* could somehow be responsible for making Drew look like an ass in front of the entire Line, she might be able to gain the acceptance she really wanted, and at the same time, maybe end the power struggle between her Captain and the drum major.

*If you do something to humiliate Drew, you can kiss off **ever** getting together with him. What guy do you know that wants a girlfriend who has publicly made him look like an idiot?*

Another voice entirely entered her mind…and it sounded a lot like Lucy's.

Here's what you do, girl…kill two birds with one stone. Go to Drew first, all wide eyed and damsel in distress and tell him you need his help. Guys are a sucker for that kind of thing.

I'm listening…

Once Drew is on board, you pull a stunt in front of J.D. and the rest of the Line. They all have a good laugh, but you haven't completely wrecked it with Drew…because he knew what was coming. He feels all warm and fuzzy because he helped out a cute girl, and the Line will have a new champion. Even J.D. won't be able to argue with you.

You honestly think Drew would do something like that for me? I'm no-one.

I disagree. I think you are definitely someone. Besides, what's the worst that can happen? He says no? Who cares? His loss.

I guess so…

You guess? Come on! Go for it. Find him tonight and talk it over. Just make sure the Line doesn't see the two of you talking or the jig is up.

Great, thought Bronwyn, my subconscious sounds like a cross between Lucy and a gangster mol, maybe the sun has finally killed all of my brain cells. Determined to do things on her own, and not contact the *real* Lucy unless absolutely necessary, the redhead knew she had to act quickly, and time at band camp was running out.

A few hours later at dinner, everyone hurried through the meal so they could scurry back to their rooms to primp for the Band Camp dance. While there were a lot of flirtations during the week, couples could make things official by dancing a few songs together that night.

Bronwyn had been nervous throughout dinner and had picked at her food, knowing she *had* to make her move tonight. All week she had longingly looked at the rest of the Line always sitting together. They hadn't told her to not sit with them, but they never specifically invited her over either.

Maybe next year…

Bronwyn kept her eye on Drew until he finally left the dining hall. It was now or never. She quickly scanned the room to make sure no one else on the Line was around before she practically sprinted over to Drew's side just outside the doors of the cafeteria.

"Hey Drew!" she gasped.

"Hey, Bronwyn."

Even though she was breathing like a marathon runner, Bronwyn smiled, realizing she liked it that Drew called her by her first name. Many in the drum line had followed J.D.'s lead and referred to her only as "Flueger" or "B," which Bronwyn thought was a bit impersonal. She liked the nickname, but wished for something that didn't totally negate her gender. Names aside, her plan to go unnoticed by the Line was immediately interrupted when she spotted some of the cymbal players coming up the path. Hesitating for only a second, she grabbed Drew's hand and pulled him in the other direction.

Drew asked, "Something you want to share?"

Bronwyn wanted to curse as her cheeks got noticeably redder.

Remember, he's just part of the plan...be cool.

With as much "coolness" as she could muster, Bronwyn stated, "So, you've probably noticed some tension this week within the Line."

"Really?"

Bronwyn paused, but awkwardly kept talking, "Well, I mean, maybe you haven't noticed but..."

Drew was grinning, "Of course I've noticed. The whole band has noticed. However, J.D. doesn't strike me as the type to call a truce."

Bronwyn gulped, but forced herself to go ahead with the plan, "What if I told you I knew a way to make things better?"

"I don't really trust that tone of voice, Bronwyn."

"Well, how about you hear me out before making any decisions? It's just going to take a little counterfeit on your part."

She decided if Drew was going to make a giant sacrifice on behalf of the greater good of the band, the least she could do was tell him the truth...even if it was pathetic. He paused, and Bronwyn wondered frantically what other plan could possibly work at this point.

Finally, he said, "Let's hear your plan then."

After pacing for a moment, she started, "Okay, here's the thing. The Line, for whatever unknown and probable masculine reason, has not fully accepted me. This fact could make for a very long season on my part. Now, I happen to love being on the Battery and I'm a good snare player, but the only way for me gain acceptance is..." Bronwyn paused, unsure how to put the words together.

"Is?" Drew prompted.

She rushed ahead, "Is to make you look like an idiot."

Obviously wondering how this plan was instrumental to the marching band's ultimate harmony, Drew opened his mouth to ask a question, but Bronwyn cut him off, continuing, "If, in J.D.'s mind, you have been properly humiliated, I think he will drop this whole competitive thing and the entire band can go back to normal. Does that any make sense?"

Drew stood still, processing and considering the information the little redhead had unloaded on him.

Bronwyn took another deep breath, and forced herself to look into Drew's blue eyes, "Please?"

Drew hesitated another second before he responded, "Alright, I'll do it."

Bronwyn was in shock. It had been too easy. "What?"

"On one condition…"

"Yes?"

"You owe me. You owe me big."

Still shocked he had agreed so easily, Bronwyn nodded, "I know."

"So, just consider that sometime I'm going to ask you for a favor and I'm going to hold you to it."

"Agreed – whatever you want!"

Drew, intrigued by her innocence, and perhaps the brilliant simplicity of her plan, continued, "So, any ideas about how to publicly embarrass me?"

Bronwyn shook her head, "I wish I had something, but honestly, I wasn't sure what you were going to say, so I didn't think that far ahead. In the meantime, let's say if I come up to you and start doing or saying something outrageous, just go along with it, okay?"

"Thanks for the warning."

During their conversation, they had walked around the entire campus and were back at the dorms. Bronwyn realized she had run out of things to say. She gestured vaguely at the girls' hall, "So, guess I'd better go get ready…"

"Yup."

"You should get ready too, wouldn't want to keep your fans waiting," Bronwyn said, unable to help herself.

"What can I say?"

"You're no better than the rest of the Line."

"See you at the dance, Bronwyn."

Bronwyn practically floated up to her room.

Megan saw the look on roommate's face and asked, "Was I seeing things, or were you just talking to Drew?"

Bronwyn smiled dreamily, "You weren't. I was."

Chapter Four

Strategery

To: karatechop@state.edu
From: FHHSsnaregrl@FHHS.edu

Lucy,

So, in an effort to fit in with the Line, I'm kind of working on this complicated plan that will involve Drew (remember him? The cute drum major who looks vaguely like Zac Efron?). Anyway, in a total un-Bronwyn like move (that I hope you would have been very proud of) I went up and asked him if he would help out…

… and he said yes!

Of course, in my crazy head, that meant he liked me and I got all excited and dressed up for the dance and then he didn't even look at me. Not once. I felt like a complete idiot. So now, I don't where I am and wondering why I even asked for his help in the first place. Is it December yet?

Seriously, I'm just ready for it to be my junior year and for both Drew and J.D. to have graduated.

Please tell me you know what I'm talking about!

B

To: FHHSsnaregrl@FHHS.edu
From: karatechop@state.edu

B,

*Yeah, I know what that's about. My freshman year on the Line, I became obsessed with a snare player named Cameron. And it **killed** me to see him talk to anyone else. I knew it was never going to happen, but my brain just wouldn't let it go… and then he moved away. Waaahhh!! But I digress, so…you just have to wait it out, either that, or find some guy who **does** notice you and go for it. Or, the worst (or best) of all, tell him how you feel. You'd have more guts than I did, I never got the chance with Cameron.*

Later Sk8er!

Lucy

P.S. I'm curious, what exactly does this plan of yours involve?

P.P.S. I'm sure this season will turn out okay – REMEMBER, YOU'RE A SNARE PLAYER!

After reading Lucy's response, Bronwyn climbed into bed. With the question of what exactly she could do weighing on her mind, she tossed and turned, trying to get to sleep. She didn't want to involve Megan and Meredith because, well, the whole idea was based on the embarrassing fact that she couldn't admit to them. Both girls were so happy and popular in their sections, they probably didn't have a concept of what it was like to watch everything from the outside. The only plan Bronwyn could think of to get back on the good side of the Line was the following scenario:

INT. Percussion Room

Enter DREW, an attractive 17-year-old male. Percussionists are busy goofing off before a practice.

DREW
(nervous)
Has anyone seen Bronwyn?

The drummers part as BRONWYN FLUEGER, our beautiful, resplendent, scarlet haired, 15 year old heroine, walks up.

BRONWYN
What do you want?

                         DREW
                  (even more anxious)
     Umm...I was wondering if you would maybe like to
                    out with me?

                        BRONWYN
                      (laughing)
                       No way.

                         DREW
                       Please?

                        BRONWYN
     Sorry, drummers like me don't date losers like
                         you.

     Drew leaves the room with a dejected and pitiful
     look on his face, while the rest of the drummers
     crowd around Bronwyn, patting her on the back.

                         J.D.
         I always knew you were one of us.
                (calling out after Drew)
                       Loser!

Bronwyn sighed.

Is that the best I can do?

It's simple and easy and there is no way the guys will not understand it. You win, he loses.

Yeah...but I don't know if he'll go along with damaging his rep just for me. I'm just some sophomore he doesn't know. What does he get out of this except complete and utter humiliation?

All you can do is ask and find out.

Still trying to get to sleep, Bronwyn wondered why her sophomore year was not going to start exactly like she had planned back in the spring. Her mental checklist had gone very much according to plan. She had earned the coveted spot on the snare line she had wanted so badly. She had classes with most of her friends. What she hadn't planned on, and couldn't have predicted, was her need for acceptance from the Line. She wanted to be included, to belong, rather than be an outsider in her own section. Was she being too sensitive? Should she just get over herself and accept the way things were?

It was a long time before she finally drifted off to sleep.

Tuesday afternoon was the first practice after band camp. Bronwyn glumly put on her drum and walked out to the field by herself. She looked at Beth and Valerie jealously. Of course, they were fitting in seamlessly with the other members of the Pit.

Some example you are setting for them, Flueger.

Looking up at the drum major podium was especially difficult. The same little voice inside of her nagged, *you think just because he agreed to help you that means anything?*

After practice, Bronwyn didn't even bother to ask Ben for a ride home – who would want someone as lame as her riding shotgun? As she was walking to the phones to call her Dad to pick her up, she heard someone approach her.

"So, you come up with our plan yet?"

Bronwyn's heart fluttered at the use of the word "our." She managed to respond, "Umm, well, actually, no, I haven't."

"Really?"

"I'm kind of stumped."

Except that's a lie, because I know exactly what I need to do, but it's going to require a lot on your part, and I'm not sure if that's what you signed up for.

They walked in silence. When Bronwyn reached the phone and dug around in her pockets for enough change to make the call, Drew looked at her strangely and asked, "What are you doing?"

"Calling my parents, because, y'know, I haven't quite mastered the art of teleporting just yet."

"Tell you what, how about I drive you home and we'll discuss the plan on the way?"

Unprepared for Drew's attention, Bronwyn looked at him skeptically and questioned, "You sure you don't have other places to go? People to see?"

"I can see them after I drop you off."

"Oh, okay, just let me call my parents and tell them I have a ride."

"Flueger, you can use my cell."

Bronwyn blushed, and replied, "Fine, Mr. Bossy, I didn't want to go around assuming things. Even if the rest of my section does not, I have manners."

As they walked to the parking lot, Bronwyn called and told her parents she would be home shortly and filled in the silence by giving Drew directions to her house. Gentleman that he was, Drew opened her side of the car first. Bronwyn got in and scrambled to open his door. The drum major got in the car smiling, and said, "Thanks, you'd be surprised how many girls forget to do that."

Bronwyn beamed back at him.

...No time like the present, you've got him in an enclosed space...

Ignoring her subconscious, she stalled and reverted to small talk, "So, how are you feeling about the show?"

As soon as she asked the question, she cringed. It was no secret the show was not turning out how anyone expected. By the end of band camp, the Forrest Hills Flyers were severely behind schedule. The arrangement, complicated drill, and addition of a third drum major had slowed down the speed of learning, leaving a frustrated and exhausted band. The continued rivalry between J.D. and Drew was not helping things.

He sighed, and Bronwyn felt her heart go out to the drum major. During practices, he was always the picture of leadership. Here in the car, she realized maybe things were affecting him more than she thought. Maybe she wasn't the only one having a difficult season.

Rather than wait for his answer, she quickly made excuses, "You know, it's not your fault."

"Isn't it?"

"Of course not! Last time I checked, there were over two hundred people on the field and each of them has a hand in the final results. Plus, dude, it's seriously early in the season..."

"This time last year—"

"Was a different show." Bronwyn remember being in the Pit and how easy her life had been. She continued softly, "Was a different everything."

"You're right about that."

"So, give it some time."

He paused, and then commented, "Sounds like maybe you should do the same."

"About what? J.D.?"

"Yup."

"That's different."

"How?"

"Trust me, it just is." Bronwyn, uncomfortable with talking about the deeper issues within her section, wanted to focus on the solution. Although she was enjoying the personal conversation and getting to know Drew better, she said abruptly, "So, um, I think you should ask me out."

He waited a few moments before he replied, "I'm confused, what does that have to do with waiting things out?"

"It doesn't."

"As long as you're sure this is the best way..."

"I am." She impatiently tapped the snare solo out on her leg.

He eyed her nervous response, but answered, "Then let's hear an explanation."

"Well, I mean, you wouldn't be asking me out for real. Basically, I had this scenario in my mind, where like, after a practice or something you come in the percussion room and you're all 'let's go out' and I'm all 'no' and then the Line is like 'she's our hero.'"

Drew was quiet; obviously, he needed a moment to process the 'plan.'

Mistaking his silence for disapproval, Bronwyn kept talking, "I know, it's stupid. Forget I asked. I guess you have a reputation to worry about."

"What's *that* supposed to mean?"

"Well, um, I don't think you've ever shown much of an interest in um, people like me."

"What are you implying?"

She replied honestly, "Basically, from what I can tell, you have a type and that sort of girl is not me. You know, maybe I overlooked the whole reality of my plan. I mean, no one would believe it if you waltzed into the percussion room and suddenly showed an interest in me. "

Drew looked in his rear view mirror and then back at the road, before he said, "I guess you're right. I do have a bit of a trend."

"So, like I said, I know it's a lot to ask for and just forget I asked. I'll come up with a new plan and you can forget I even asked."

They were quiet the rest of the way to Bronwyn's house. As Drew pulled up, and the sophomore went to immediately get out of the car, more than ready for the entire painful experience to be over, Drew placed his hand on her smaller one, "Wait."

Bronwyn looked up at him, "Yes?"

"I think I figured out a way this just might work."

"And?"

"It's kind of your idea and kind of like that movie with Freddie Prinze Jr."

"You mean *She's All That*? You've seen *She's All That*?" Bronwyn smirked.

"Hey, do you want to hear the plan or not?"

"I do."

"The thing is, I don't think your idea is enough, basically, it needs something more. So, here's what I'm thinking – I'll mention, loudly, in front of one of the members of the Line that I'm interested in asking you to, let's say, Homecoming or something. That information will get back to J.D., who being the guy I think he is, will come up to me and make some sort of wager as to whether or not you will say yes. When you say no, then J.D. feels like a star and you get the support of the Line and I will…well, I guess I'll go back to dating the girls I usually date."

"Do you think that would actually work?" Even after spending an entire summer with five teenage boys, Bronwyn realized she was really no closer to understanding the male gender than she was a year ago.

"I'm a guy, aren't I? I think I would know better what works and what doesn't."

"And you're sure you want to go through with this?"

Drew shrugged his shoulders, "Why not? My senior year was going to be boring otherwise."

"Well, then, if that's the case, then I have the perfect person you can 'comment' to," Bronwyn said, a devious grin on her face.

At the same time, at a post-practice gathering at Waffle House, the rest of the snare section were having a conversation of their own. Adam picked at his hash browns, and said, "This doesn't feel right."

J.D. looked over at him and asked sarcastically, "What do you mean? Are your hash browns not to made to golden perfection?"

Adam rolled his eyes and answered, "I'm not talking about that. Listen, it's not that I don't love our section and all, it's just…"

Kevin asked, "It's just what?"

Adam sighed, "I can't believe I'm actually saying this, but I think we're being really shitty to Bronwyn."

J.D. scoffed, "Who, Flueger? Are you kidding?"

Scott said, "Why do you care, Adam? Something going on of your side of the snare line we should know about?"

Lance interrupted, "Cut him some slack, guys. I'm on the other side of Adam and I think I would know if something was going on."

J.D. asked, "Does that mean you're on her side?"

Lance crossed his arms, "There should be no 'sides' on the snare line, J.D."

J.D. glared at Lance, "Are you telling me how to run my Line?"

Adam broke the tension and said, "Seriously J.D., all I'm trying to say is I think Bronwyn is starting to take it personally that we never include her in anything."

J.D. looked around the table and asked, "Do you remember your first year on the Battery?"

Kevin replied, "Yeah man, I marched with Lucy on the bass line, it was a laugh a minute in our section."

J.D. gave him a stern look, "You're not helping."

Scott said, "Maybe you're right, I mean we really came together at band camp, but it was as the five of us. Our section has six people in it."

Lance nodded and added, "Seriously, I mean what we do and how we act sets the precedent for the rest of the Line, and right now, we're setting a bad example."

J.D. shrugged, "I guess. Fine, I will *try* and be nicer to Flueger."

Happy with their Captain's attempt at normalcy, Adam smiled and said, "You won't regret it. Plus, I think once we include her, it's really going to help us as a section."

Chapter Five

Operation Tattletale

Bronwyn nodded to Drew from across the field. It was two weeks into the school year and today they were going to set 'The Plan' in motion. It was weird, because in the past week, Bronwyn had actually noticed a slight difference in how her section were treating her. Sure, she usually spent breaks hanging with her band friends and not the Line, but while she couldn't put her finger on it, it was as if they were actually being a little nicer to her. Furthermore, Ben decided his earlier comment of "anytime" meant he didn't mind taking Bronwyn home from practice on Tuesdays and Thursdays and even picking her up for Friday night games.

Now is not the time to hesitate, as much as I'd like to think I'm one of them, the plan will ensure my acceptance!

Bronwyn could only wait and hope J.D. would take the bait and react accordingly. She was also nervous because they had to involve another person. She didn't want Operation Tattletale somehow getting out to the rest of the band, but she trusted her friend Pete, a trumpet player.

Drew found Pete after practice, "You ready for this?"

Pete smiled, "Well, Bronwyn's a good friend and if you two think this will work…"

"It will."

"There he is now, I'll see you in a few."

Pete planted himself directly behind Bronwyn's favorite person in the section, Tony Clarke, as he walked back from the practice field to the percussion room.

Drew jogged up and joined Pete, then asked, "Hey man, you gotta sec?"

"What's up?"

"So…you're friends with Bronwyn, aren't you?"

"Yeah, why?"

"Do you know if she's dating anyone right now?" Drew asked loudly.

It was all Tony could do not to turn around. He visibly slowed his pace so he was walking closer to the pair behind him.

"No, she's not. Why are you asking?"

"No reason."

"Really?"

"Well…you promise to keep this to yourself?"

"Sure."

"I was thinking about asking her to Homecoming."

Tony almost tripped over himself. Pete, noticing Tony's antics, had to hold back a laugh, "Seriously?"

"You think she would say yes?"

"I'm not sure. Maybe you should just ask and find out."

"Yeah…although, I think I may wait awhile and get to know her a little better."

"Do you want me to let her know that you're interested? I can drop some hints for you."

Drew said quickly, "No! I mean, not for now, let's just keep it between you and me."

"No worries."

At that point Tony peeled off and went zooming in the direction of the band room. Drew clapped Pete on the back and said, "Do you think he bought it?"

"Hook, line, and sinker. I'm sure J.D. will know about your 'intentions' in the next ten minutes."

"Great, thanks for your help."

Still slightly confused about what was actually going on, Pete commented vaguely, "I hope things work out the way you want it to."

Tony half sprinted into the percussion room. He quickly found J.D. and pulled his Captain aside, "Hey dude, I have something to tell you."

The tone of Tony's voice made J.D. pay immediate attention. He told the younger drummer, "Alright, put your drum away and let's talk outside."

They walked quietly into the hall. J.D. crossed his arms, and asked, "What's this all about, Tony?"

"You know Drew?"

"Our dumb major?"

"Yeah, him."

"What about him?"

Tony looked around to see if anyone was listening. Satisfied they weren't, he commented, "It seems as though he's taken interest in Bronwyn."

"As in Flueger?"

The sophomore rolled his eyes, "You know another Bronwyn?"

"Continue."

"Apparently, he's thinking of asking her to Homecoming."

"And how do you know all this?"

"I overheard Drew talking to one of Bronwyn's friends."

"Curious."

Tony questioned him, "Are you going to do anything about it? Do you think she would actually say yes?"

J.D. smirked, "Not sure yet, but it does give me a few ideas to keep things interesting this season. Do me a favor and make sure to keep this to yourself, okay?"

"Sure thing, J.D," Tony said proudly.

Drew was not surprised when he saw J.D. waiting at his car that evening. The drum major had to wipe the smile from his face before J.D. knew something was up. Dumping his book bag in the trunk, he asked gruffly, "Can I help you?"

J.D. crossed his arms and said, "I hear you're interested in someone in my section."

"Who told you that?"

"So it's true? I don't hear you denying anything."

Drew shrugged and responded, "Well, sort of."

"And you want to ask her to Homecoming?" Given there were only three young women in the entire section, there was no need to mention the "her" by name.

Drew kicked a tire, "I'm going to kill—"

J.D. grinned evilly, "Listen, don't ask how I know. I have my sources. I was wondering if you wanted to make a bit of a side bet on the situation?"

"I don't like the sound of this…"

"Trust me, Bronwyn never has to know. Just a gentleman's wager."

"That's pretty low, J.D., even for you."

"She won't find out. Anyway, what do you care? You'll be at college next year and not worried about some pathetic high school girl."

Drew waited a moment before asking, "Alright, I'll consider it. What are the odds?"

"She says yes…I'll personally pay for your entire 'delightful' Homecoming evening together."

"Sounds good."

"She says no…you admit personally to my section that you have no leadership abilities or any sort of dominance over them."

"Isn't it bad enough that she will say no?"

"Nope."

Drew scuffed his shoe on the pavement, "Let me think about the terms. In the mean time, do not tell *anyone* the plan. If I find out that Bronwyn or anyone else in your section knows…everything is off. *Comprende?*"

"Yeah, just don't keep me waiting." J.D. walked off towards his own car.

As soon as the snare player was out of sight, Drew called Bronwyn and hoped that she was home. When he heard her voice, he said, "It worked."

"He actually bought it?"

"Sure did. So, if I 'win' he's going to spring for our entire Homecoming night."

Bronwyn didn't know how to respond. While she was glad Drew had been able to accurately predict how things were going to go, she was also a bit sad J.D. would so eagerly bet on her. Finally, she said lightly, "Awww…too bad for 'us,' I guess."

Drew laughed, "Yeah, I guess so, and when I lose, I have to admit to the Line that I don't have any control over them blah, blah."

"J.D. certainly knows how to play hardball, doesn't he?"

"Yeah, I don't mind so much. As long as I'm telling just the Line and not the entire band, then I think we'll all be a big happy family again and then we can go onto winning some competitions this season."

"Thanks again."

"Hey, no big deal. With the show going the way it is, it will be a nice distraction. I'm sure by next week it will be old news."

"Well, thanks for calling and letting me know. Night, Drew."

"Night, Bronwyn."

Bronwyn hung up the phone and sighed.

What were you hoping for? A happy ending?

No…but, I wish I could've gone on at least one date.

Are you sure that's it?

Bronwyn trudged up to her room, not wanting to admit the real reason she was sad. Deep down, she'd held the hope that maybe Drew would warm up to the idea of actually going out with her, that maybe she would be more than just a 'distraction' during his senior year.

Friday was the first home game of the season. The stands were packed and Bronwyn was excited about her first night marching with the Battery. All the hours of practice that had led up to the show so far were about to pay off. Rehearsals were one thing, but it was something else entirely to march on the field in front of the crowd. This game was especially unique, because tonight the Forrest Hills Flyers were revealing their new uniforms. Bronwyn couldn't believe her luck – the uniform had not been updated in six seasons but this year they were given sleek, new designs.

As Mr. Izzo gathered the section leaders on the track after the National Anthem, Drew caught up with J.D. and said in a low tone, "Fine. We'll do things your way."

They both looked over at Bronwyn, who was finding her way up in the stands. She had a fierce grin on her face and looked delighted to be a part of the section.

J.D. asked, "When were you thinking about asking her?"

"The sooner the better. And you're sure you haven't told anyone?"

J.D. put his hands up, "I promise. This is just between you and her… and me."

Drew rolled his eyes, but replied, "May the best man win."

Bronwyn, excited as she was to be sitting among the snares in the stands, couldn't help but notice her Captain and drum major discussing something at the bottom of the stands. Tony also noted with interest that the two were talking.

Once secure on the drum major podium, Drew's eyes sought Bronwyn's as he lifted his hands for the crowd pleasing stands song "Hey Baby." He winked. Bronwyn knew that was the cue that he was going to set the plan in action.

Although she had played a reasonably clean performance, Bronwyn knew the band still had a long way to go before they would be ready for competition. During the second song, when the band was facing backfield for an extended move, J.D. had sped up the tempo, blazing almost three measures ahead of the rest of the band. Bronwyn still wasn't sure how they had all ended together. As Drew had brought his hands down, he glared in the direction of the Line. She wondered if he would still show up tonight.

Bronwyn tried to act as normal as possible as she put her drum away and waited for Drew to arrive. They had originally decided it would be best if as many people from the Line saw them leave together. Bronwyn was talking to Adam when she felt a tap on her shoulder. She turned around and looked up to see Drew. She asked as casually as possible, "Yes?"

"I was wondering if, I, uh, could talk to you."

"Sure, what's up?" Bronwyn asked brightly, knowing his presence in the percussion room would start the band rumor mill churning. As each section of the band had 'their' specific territory, it was rare to see a lot of cross over between the groups. More often than not, the drum majors hung out in the band director's office or with their previous section. Given the ongoing rivalry between J.D. and Drew, and the somewhat disastrous performance earlier in the evening, the drum major could just as easily be in the drummer's territory to have a word with the Captain. It made his interest in the sophomore snare that more interesting.

"Well, um, can I give you a ride home?"

Bronwyn pretended to consider for a moment before she replied, "That would be fine. Let me just get my stuff."

It took Bronwyn about two seconds to grab her bag. She tucked her arm under Drew's, "Let's go."

It was probably a first, but the percussion room was silent as the pair left together. As soon as they were in the hall, Bronwyn whooped with nervous laughter. What had a few weeks ago been a crazy idea was now actually happening. In response, Drew smiled. It was good to see the sophomore in such a great mood. After the "attention" incident outside of the dining hall on the first day of band camp, he had unexpectedly started keeping his eye on her. Although she tried to hide it, Bronwyn usually had a distant look on her face. Tonight, however, her blue grey eyes were lit up and she had a smile that almost split her face.

As they walked outside towards the parking lot, Drew said, "Well, we might as well play up the charade for a little while."

Bronwyn nodded, "The more they think you like me, the better it will be when I tell you 'no.'"

Drew pretended to look crushed, "How will I ever survive?"

Inside the car, Bronwyn asked, "Hey Drew?"

"Yes?"

"I was thinking we might tweak things a little bit."

"What more could we do?"

Bronwyn took a deep breath and blurted out, "I want a trial date."

Drew raised his eyebrows.

Before he had a chance to say no, Bronwyn rushed ahead, "See, here's the thing. Hypothetically, I don't think I would just say yes, just because, you know? I mean Homecoming is a big decision and one I don't think I can make unless I really know the guy..." She trailed off, hoping he would understand.

Drew smiled and asked, "Bronwyn, are you asking me on a date?"

Bronwyn gulped and played with a strand of her hair, "Umm, is that what it sounds like I'm doing?"

"That's exactly what it sounds like."

Bronwyn's face got red, and her heart started beating very hard.

Why are you stressing?

Not sure.

He says yes, he says no. You weren't even this nervous at your auditions.

Drumming, I know. Boys, I do not.

He still hasn't said anything.

Don't remind me.

Drew looked out the window and said, "You know, girls have done a lot of things to get my attention in the past, but no one has been as sneaky as you have. Was this all some elaborate scheme to get a date with me? Are you playing all of us?"

Bronwyn's heart was sinking in her chest and she finally croaked, "No."

"You promise?"

Bronwyn scratched a tiny piece of lint on her shorts and murmured, "Forget I asked. We'll just stick the original plan."

Not a moment too soon, they pulled up to Bronwyn's house. She managed to squeak out, "Night, Drew. Thanks for the ride."

"Night, Bronwyn."

As Bronwyn got out of the car, Drew almost called her back, but then put his car into gear and pulled away, thoughts instantly filling his head.

Good going, idiot.

What?

There are easier and nicer ways to turn a girl down, you know.

I wasn't—

You actually think she planned this whole thing?! The truth is much simpler than that.

Yeah, what is it?

Bronwyn Flueger has all the normal, healthy signs of having a crush on you.

Drew turned up the music in his car, unsure how to process that information.

Chapter Six

Boys Will Be Boys

On Monday, Bronwyn strolled into fifth period as if everything in her life was completely normal and that she had not left the sanctuary of the percussion room on Friday night with the drum major. Even though she felt terrible and even worse off than when she started this crazy adventure, Bronwyn forced a smug smile on her face.

Might as well keep them guessing...

Although he would never admit to it, J.D. had been waiting for Bronwyn. However, he couldn't tell what answer she had given Drew based on her expression. He was also going to be damned if he ran up to her like a giddy schoolgirl asking if she had said "yes" to Drew's pressing question that he wasn't even supposed to know about. Nor was the Captain of the drum line going to call the drum major over the weekend and get that answer. J.D. walked over to Tony, "Hey man, I need you to do something for me."

Tony, always looking for a way to get 'in' with the upperclassmen in the section, asked, "What's up?"

"I need you to go ask Bronwyn something."

"What is it?"

"Umm...this is going to sound weird, but you ask her how things went with Drew?"

Tony looked at his Captain strangely, "Well..."

"Well what?"

"She and I aren't the best of friends."

"Hmph."

"I mean; she's just going to wonder why I'm coming up and asking her such a random question. Why do you want to know anyway?"

"I have my reasons."

His thoughts on something entirely non-percussion, J.D. began the warm up. Since Bronwyn was on his far left; he couldn't look at her for the entire class. He guessed she had said no.

"So?" Meredith asked on the way down to the practice field.

"So, what?" Bronwyn responded, oblivious.

"Aren't you going to tell us how things went with Drew?" Meredith looked at Megan, and continued, "We kind of thought you would tell us over the weekend."

"Oh that."

"Yes – that," Megan said.

"Well, he drove me home. End of story. No big deal."

"Sure, the hottest senior in the band, who just also happens to be the drum major, drives you home and that's it? 'No big deal?'" Megan asked skeptically. "Isn't this the same guy you've been crushing on for almost a year?"

"It's not relevant."

Meredith blinked rapidly, and ignoring Bronwyn's attempts to avoid the subject, questioned, "What did you guys talk about?"

"You know, stuff."

Meredith sighed and asked, "Is there something you're not telling us? Is this some sort of weird truce attempt? Did J.D. put you up to it?"

If they only knew…

What would they say?

That I'm crazy.

Bronwyn snapped, "Look, it was just one ride. Maybe it's some sort of underclassmen outreach program, I'm not entirely sure. All I know is that it was definitely a one time thing. So, can we just drop it please?"

Her friends exchanged worried glances. They knew this season was stressing out Bronwyn more than last year, but her reaction was concerning. For all the jokes they made about her red hair and temper to match, for the most part, Bronwyn was the most level headed among them. This response was out of character.

Meredith let the topic drop – for now – and linked an arm with the snare drummer, "If you say so."

Her friends concern only made things worse. As she walked towards where the Line was gathering, Bronwyn knew she should feel happier. Drew and J.D. were going to have their little talk, J.D. was going to feel like he was the big winner and she would finally have the acceptance she desperately wanted from the Line.

I guess I got greedy.

Don't think like that. One date hardly counts as being greedy.

Well, I might be winning the acceptance of the Line, but now Drew thinks I'm some sort of conniving bitch. Why did I even ask him to begin with?

You win some; you lose some.
I think we all know who the loser is here.

Drew noticed Bronwyn purposely avoiding him and wasn't surprised. He was also not shocked to find J.D. sitting at his car after practice. The drum major commented sarcastically, "People are going to start thinking we're a couple, J.D."

"Hardly."

"I'm guessing this is not a courtesy call."

"Well, the *entire* Line saw you two leave together on Friday."

"Why does that mean anything?"

"Did you ask her?"

Drew suppressed a grin. He knew he would lose face later when he had to tell J.D. that Bronwyn had said "no," but somehow everything was worth it hearing the tough, disciplined drum line Captain say, 'Did you ask her?'

"I did."

"You are deliberately not making this easy on me."

"So quick to catch on, Strauss."

J.D. crossed his arms, then played what he thought was his trump card, "You know I can just go and tell Flueger what we're up to. I'm sure she wouldn't be happy to learn you sold her out."

At J.D.'s response, Drew hesitated a moment longer, then decided he had to screw with the percussion section leader for a bit longer. He replied, "Well, if you must know, I did ask her and she said she couldn't make that decision until she went on a date with me."

"She did what?!"

"So I said yes."

"This wasn't part of the bargain."

"Look, it's not as if I had any choice. Do you think Bronwyn just woke up on Friday morning and decided she would mess up our whole deal?"

"No," said J.D. glumly.

"Well, I'm going to try and be my charming best and you can just sit tight."

"I guess."

"Still so sure you're going to win?"

J.D., who didn't like to be challenged, responded instantly, "I'm so sure, I'll throw in a limo if you *do* win!"

Two days later, at Thursday's practice, Bronwyn was walking back towards the school with Megan and Meredith, trying to convince them she was back to 'normal,' when someone behind her asked, "You got a minute?"

Bronwyn's heart fluttered for a moment, then sank like a rock; she would recognize that voice anywhere. She responded, "Sure."

Her friends exchanged approving looks as Bronwyn hung back to walk down with Drew.

"So, I talked to J.D."

Bronwyn sighed, "When are you going to make your big announcement?"

"After our date."

Drew's statement caused Bronwyn to trip over her own feet. She reached out blindly to keep from falling and caught herself on the senior's strong forearm. The close contact with her crush made her cheeks burn and she said, "I'm sorry, I thought you said 'after we go on our date.'"

"I did."

They walked in silence. Bronwyn gathered her courage and asked, "What changed your mind?"

"I wanted to mess with J.D. a little longer."

"Oh." Bronwyn tried her best to keep the disappointment out of her voice.

Drew continued, "And, I have to admit, I was a little curious what it would be like to go out with the cute drummer prodigy everyone keeps talking about."

"Oh." Bronwyn tried her best to keep the smile out of her voice.

"So, catch you later?"

"Sure," Bronwyn managed to choke out.

Bronwyn watched Drew walk away and wasn't sure what the next part in the equation was. From all the experiences and scenarios she had known, it was usually so much easier and direct. Boy likes girl, boy asks girl out, boy and girl go on date. Boy and girl become boyfriend and girlfriend. Her situation had completely deviated from the norm: girl has major crush on boy, girl asks boy to help with messed up scheme to get girl's drum line to respect her, girl semi-asks out boy, boy appears to say no but then says yes? Bronwyn smiled, not exactly sure how everything added up to this point, but overall happy with the end results.

Ben was waiting for her in the percussion room, "Ready to go?"

Bronwyn carefully put her drum in its slot, "Yup."

They walked out to the parking lot. Ben asked, "So what's up with you and that drum major guy?"

Bronwyn looked at Ben as if he had just asked her how to play the bass clarinet, "What are you talking about?"

"I just noticed he was talking to you, that's all."

Bronwyn smiled to herself, it was true, guys were just as bad as girls when it came to all things gossip. She replied, "Nothing really, I guess."

"Well, let me know if he does anything out of line, I got your back. I have to look out for my shotgun buddy, after all."

To: karatechop@state.edu
From: FHHSsnaregrl@FHHS.edu

Lucy!!!!

I am so freaking out here. So, I got myself into a weird situation, and now I'm more or less accidentally going out with Drew. On a date!!! At least I think we are – I'm not quite sure. I have no idea how to act or what to do. Help please!!

Awkwardly (turtle) yours,

B

To: FHHSsnaregrl@FHHS.edu
From: karatechop@state.edu

Bronwyn,

How do you 'accidentally' date someone? Okay, that's weird. I know it's been said a million times before, but just be YOURSELF. I'm guessing Drew has been on a date before, so let him take the lead and just relax. Also, if you have a cute dog to bring along, that usually helps break the ice.

Finally, although I think it's fairly obvious, I have to ask, do you really like him? I want details as soon as this thing is over!!

Best,

Lucy

To: karatechop@state.edu
From: FHHSsnaregrl@FHHS.edu

Lucy,

Sometimes it's hard to just be myself, because most days I'm not really sure who that girl is...

And yes, I really do like him. That's the problem…J.D. doesn't like him.

B

At his house, while distracting himself from various college applications, Drew tried to come up with something creative for his one date with Bronwyn. No pressure there. He wasn't exactly sure what he and Bronwyn were going to end up doing, but seeing her eyes light up like they did when he told her they were going out, he knew it would be worth it.

What in the hell have I gotten myself into?

Do you really mind that much going out with her?

No…but I still think that she planned this whole thing.

You really can't buy into the fact that the girl just might actually like you?

She must be doing something to trick me; I've never felt this way about—

Hold up, were you about to admit that you might have feelings for her?

No…maybe, and anyway, it's all over after this date. Then I go to J.D. and she gets acceptance from the Line and I go back to my regularly scheduled season.

Just keep telling yourself that.

To: FHHSsnaregrl@FHHS.edu
From: karatechop@state.edu

Bronwyn,

So I was thinking it over and I don't want you to make a mistake that I made. Please, please, tell me that you've told someone else about your crazy plans. Sometimes your friends can surprise you in amazing ways. I'll bet you've got some people on your side…so go to those girls (or guys) and talk it out. You'll be glad you did.

Luce

Bronwyn read Lucy's words and realized she had been keeping this situation to herself for too long. When she had conceived the plan at band camp, she hadn't actually believed it would get as far as it did. Maybe there was also a small part of her that thought everything would fall apart if she told someone. However, more than anything, she desperately needed some outside opinions. She immediately got on the phone with Megan and Meredith and planned some emergency girl time the following day.

Chapter Seven

Facing the Music

At Meredith's house the next afternoon, Bronwyn looked at her friends and blurted, "I'm going on date with Drew!"

Her friends looked at her as if she had sprouted wings. Megan finally found her voice and asked, "As in the same guy you told us there was 'nothing going on' with?"

Bronwyn looked at the ground, and answered, "That's the one."

Meredith asked, "Wait, how? And more importantly, *when* did all this happen?"

Bronwyn took a deep breath, then rushed ahead, "Well, see, it was around band camp when I decided I needed a scheme to get my section to like me."

Megan and Meredith exchanged a look. Meredith exclaimed, "Band camp?! And you're just telling us now? Bronwyn Margaret Flueger, just what in the hell has gotten into you?"

Bronwyn didn't have a good response for that. Instead, she twisted her hair nervously and replied, "I didn't want to get you two involved because I never thought things would get this far."

Megan, a bit more calmly, answered, "Uh, earth to Bronwyn? I think there's something bigger that you're missing here – they *do* like you."

Bronwyn shook her head and asked, "You girls were at band camp, right? I wasn't feeling a lot of love then."

Megan said, "It may have been weird then, but now, I get the feeling it's different somehow. Maybe you're just not seeing it."

Knowing of J.D.'s 'secret' bet with Drew, Bronwyn brushed the comment off and said, "I guess not. What I do know is that J.D. will think I'm awesome for turning down Drew, and everyone will like me!"

Meredith and Megan exchanged another doubtful look. This time Megan said, "Do you really think that will work?"

Bronwyn tried to keep the despair out of her voice, "It has to!"

The girls were quiet for a moment, torn between wanting to help their friend, and needing to show her that what she was feeling was mostly in her head. Finally, Meredith tried to lighten the situation by asking, "And you're *sure* there were no ulterior motives?"

Bronwyn, unable to look at her friends, turned her head and answered, "You girls don't know what it's like to be in my section. Sure, on the surface it looks great…lots of cute guys and we get to make lots of loud noises and I'm never happier than when I'm drumming, but honestly, it's been pretty lonely. I really want this season to be one I look back on and remember. I'm so sick of being on the outside!"

Bronwyn didn't realize how much the emotions had actually been building up and was surprised to find tears in her eyes. Megan rubbed Bronwyn's shoulder sympathetically and said, "Are you sure it wouldn't have been best if you had just told them how you feel?"

Bronwyn laughed bitterly, "Yeah right. There's no crying in drum line."

Meredith smiled, "You don't have to cry about it. Maybe just slip a comment in here or there."

Bronwyn said darkly, "Just so it can get back to Tony that I want to be 'popular' in my section? I don't think so."

Megan forced a smile on her face, "Well, I guess you know best then."

After a moment, Meredith added sarcastically, "And if you think going out with the drum major is the best way…well, then good for you."

Bronwyn gave them a watery smile, "Thanks for understanding, girls."

The trio got to the band room early that night. Bronwyn told Meredith and Megan she would see them at halftime and headed towards the percussion room, passing Drew on the way. He was talking to one of his senior friends, but stopped and said, "Hey, look for me after the game?"

Bronwyn nodded shyly, "Okay."

In a bit of a daze, she collected Stewie and walked out to where the band gathered to march down to the field. Henry was waiting patiently outside. Strangely enough, Bronwyn had never really talked to him alone before. He was the definition of intimidating. His abilities were some Bronwyn could only dream of having. Taking a quick look around, the redhead decided this would be a good opportunity to strike up a conversation.

"Um, hey, Henry?"

"What's up, Bronwyn?"

"Not much."

They stood for a moment, watching the rest of the band file out to the parking lot. Henry smiled in her direction and said, "If J.D. doesn't tell you enough, you're doing an awesome job."

"Really?" Bronwyn rarely heard this kind of compliment from her Instructor.

"Yup, you're actually one of the strongest players in the section. So, don't stress about those guys, they'll come around eventually."

Bronwyn looked at him skeptically, "You think?"

"It's going to take a little more maturity on their part, but just wait, I think by November you'll be surprised."

Henry peeled off a lick on Bronwyn's snare, which she automatically repeated back to him. She scuffed her black Drillmaster on the ground and said, "Henry?"

"Yup?"

"Thanks for treating me like everyone else."

"Anytime."

Bronwyn marched down to the game feeling a lot better about her life. If Henry thought she was one of the strongest players in the section, well, nothing else really mattered. Her spirits were further lifted by the evening itself – the weather was quite warm, there was plenty of goofing around in the stands, and while the show still had a way to go, as a whole it was the best version marched yet. Bronwyn almost managed to forget that she was supposed to talk to Drew after the game.

Back in the percussion room, the redhead was busy peeling off her sweaty uniform when she felt a tap on her shoulder, "Bronwyn?"

She turned around to meet Drew's sky blue eyes, and was completely embarrassed that he had caught her undressing. Bronwyn was glad she had decided to skip out on wearing the usual band t-shirt and khaki shorts this evening, optioning for her favorite black tank top and a comfy pair of grey terrycloth shorts instead.

"Yes?"

"Ready to go?"

The drummers in the room were only a little less shocked at having the drum major in their room this week. Bronwyn couldn't keep quiet for very long as they walked out. She asked, "Where are we going?"

"Can't tell you."

"Can't tell me, or won't tell me?"

"Yes."

Bronwyn giggled, "That's not an answer."

The sophomore used Drew's cell phone on the way out to his car to call her parents and tell them she was "going out with friends and that she would be home before her curfew." Bronwyn had done her best to whisper the conversation so that Drew wouldn't overhear her, but obviously had not succeeded.

"Just friends, huh?"

Bronwyn was glad it was dark out because she turned as red as her hair, "Whatever. Am I dressed for wherever we're going?"

Drew looked her over appreciatively, "You'll do."

Bronwyn flushed even more. Drew put his car in gear and pulled out of the Forrest Hills parking lot.

This is definitely starting to feel like a date.

Quit freaking out! You're only going to get one shot with this guy anyway.

Please don't remind me.

Bronwyn stared out the window and saw a number of familiar places rush by.

He's probably going to take me somewhere where no one will recognize us. He's probably embarrassed to be seen with me.

Bronwyn's once great idea now seemed like one destined to end in an embarrassing failure.

Drew reached over and squeezed her hand, "We're almost there."

When the car pulled into someone's driveway, she asked nervously, "Drew, where are we? Do you know who lives here?"

"Relax, this is my house."

"So now what?" Bronwyn was confused.

Drew looked at her and smiled, "Come on."

He led Bronwyn to his backyard and announced, "It's not my best idea ever, but it's all I could come up with on such short notice."

Bronwyn saw a large trampoline in front of her and was a bit bewildered. He continued, "I have to go in and get a few things, will you be okay out here?"

She nodded, unsure what the appropriate response should be. Drew went inside and Bronwyn nervously went ahead and got up on the trampoline and tried to come up with the right position to sit in. Eventually, she sat crossed legged and leaned back on hands, pleased the nice weather had persisted. The temperature was warm and the stars were shining brightly overhead.

Drew came out and joined her on the trampoline, easily visible to her in the almost full moon. He announced, "Come here woman, I have brought sustenance."

Bronwyn burst out with a nervous giggle. Suddenly, she was very aware of where she was sitting in proximity to Drew and tried to remind herself she had sat closer to him in the car. He didn't seem to notice her nervousness as he pulled out some snacks and started spreading them out on the bouncy surface. Bronwyn was even more impressed when he revealed an iPod attached to small speakers. For a spur of the moment date, she was delighted with his effort and somewhat relieved he hadn't taken her somewhere traditional. The thought of dinner and a movie seemed less personal than the intimate setting on the moonlit trampoline.

"Let's see, do you want Dr. Pepper or Mountain Dew?"

Bronwyn grinned; it was like being on the drum line bus. She answered carefully, "Dr. Pepper."

"Fine, Mountain Dew for me. And since we both marched a difficult show tonight, I brought grapes, cheese, and crackers to eat."

"Crackers on a trampoline? Isn't that a little messy?" Bronwyn teased.

"Umm…we'll just bounce off the crumbs."

Bronwyn laughed again and wondered if he showed this side of himself to everyone. While they ate, they discussed the show that evening and the improvements that had been made since band camp. At the end of the day, her nerves were a bit unfounded, he was very easy to talk to, and the conversation flowed between them. Wiping his mouth, Drew asked, "Finished?"

Bronwyn didn't want to be. She figured the date would be over once she was. She replied slowly, "Yes…"

"Good. Now come over here by me."

Bronwyn was suddenly shy, "Why?"

"Just come on."

She scooted carefully over to Drew's side and asked, "Are you going to take me home now?"

"Are you kidding? I'm trying to convince you to be my date for Homecoming, aren't I?"

"Yes?"

"Well, I'd hope I had more planned than Dr. Pepper. No, we're going to do some stargazing."

Bronwyn had no other dating experience to go on, but looking up at the stars sounded like a great idea to her. Drew unfurled a fleece blanket that he had brought with him, and laid it down in the middle of the trampoline.

"Hey now – there's no need to be shy." He patted the space next to him and said, "We're co-conspirators, remember?"

Bronwyn had a moment of serious panic, then decided she had better use this time for all it was worth because she wasn't sure when something remotely like this would happen to her again. Bronwyn carefully lay down next to Drew, so that she was close, but not touching him.

Drew let out a frustrated sigh, "I promise I don't bite."

Bronwyn scooted a tiny bit closer, and Drew scooted the rest of the way, putting his arm under Bronwyn's head and drawing her close to his broad chest. In a way she couldn't describe, it felt right being cuddled up next to him. She listened to the contented beat of his heart below her cheek and to the cicadas buzz in the distance. Taking a deep breath, she realized he had taken the time to splash on some cologne while he was inside getting their food. Bronwyn was almost too nervous to breathe, let alone carry on a conversation. However, it didn't seem like words were necessary on this evening in September. Drew gently stroked her hair and she wished the moment could last forever. The fall sky shone brilliantly down on them, and Bronwyn wondered why she had never done this before.

Too soon, Drew said quietly, "It's probably time to get you home."

Bronwyn sighed, but took his hand as he helped her off the trampoline. He continued holding her hand as they walked over to his car. The ride home was quiet and the radio played softly. Bronwyn was dreading the end of this car ride. It had been magical out on the trampoline, but the harsh reality that it was going to be their only date definitely put a damper on things, at least in Bronwyn's opinion. She cringed as Drew turned into her neighborhood.

Guess I won't be getting that elusive first kiss after all...

Bronwyn had long ago made up some random guy she had met on some beach vacation beach so that Meredith and Megan would stop bothering her about this whole kissing thing. She had been hoping it would be with someone meaningful.

So what if I'm a late bloomer?

Drew's voice snapped her out of her thoughts, "We're here."

Bronwyn gathered together her uniform bag and said, "Thanks for everything. I guess you'll talk to J.D. next week..."

"Yeah."

"Well, for what it matters," Bronwyn gulped, "I would've loved to go with you."

"It would've been fun."

Bronwyn's mind screeched to a stop.

Does that mean he actually might've gone with me?

She got out of the car and walked to the door, only turning around to wave goodbye, not wanting Drew to see the silly disappointed tears in her eyes.

How did you think this was going to end?

She was so lost in her own thoughts she didn't hear Drew close the car door. Bronwyn squeaked when she realized Drew was right behind her. She turned and looked up at him, his handsome face, so familiar to her now, and held her breath.

"Since it's a real date..." Drew quickly closed the distance between them. He cupped her face sweetly and lowered his mouth to her slightly open lips.

The redhead didn't have anything else to judge how great a kisser Drew was, but in her mind, it was one of the best moments in her life. When the embrace finished, she opened her eyes and saw Drew grinning at her.

"I wish things were different, Bronwyn."

"I know; me too."

"Sweet dreams."

As Drew walked away, Bronwyn briefly entertained the idea of transferring to a different school just so she could date the guy she liked. Once inside, the redhead immediately called Meredith and Megan to fill them in on the exciting news. They were both happy for her, and tried to make her feel better that she had at least gotten something special out of this whole mess.

Chapter Eight

Perhaps, Perhaps, Perhaps

J.D. approached Drew after practice on Tuesday and said, "Alright dude, she's had to have made up her mind by now."

"She did."

"And?"

"You win."

J.D. immediately burst into scornful laughter, "I always knew I liked that girl."

Drew sighed, and surprising himself, said, "I did too."

"Don't tell me you actually had feelings for her. She's just some silly sophomore."

"Is that all you see?"

J.D. didn't respond.

"Look, if that's what you think about her, I feel sorry for your section."

J.D. crossed his arms, "Don't even think about going there. I am the drum line Captain and we are doing fine this year."

Drew rolled his eyes, "Whatever. Now, I want you to listen to me for two seconds. Bronwyn may just be 'some sophomore' to you, but she's a damn good player and has done nothing to earn your resentment and exclusion. You're sabotaging your own section with your actions. Do you think any other section leader goes around betting on the people they are supposed to lead?"

"They do things their way, I do things mine."

"Just think about what I said."

"Not likely. Look, I'll expect your apology to the Line before this week's game."

"And what of Bronwyn?"

"The only thing she has going for her is that she was smart enough to turn you down."

Drew watched as J.D. walked away and felt terrible for the little redhead.

The senior drum major walked down to the practice field with Bronwyn on Thursday. He walked next to her but Bronwyn quickly noticed he wasn't saying much. She nudged him, "What's up?"

"I told J.D."

Even though she knew the plan was coming to an end, Bronwyn slumped and asked, "What did he say?"

Drew clenched his teeth and forced himself to remain calm, "Nothing. I'm going to 'talk' to you guys before Friday night's game."

Bronwyn blasted a rim shot off on her snare drum in frustration, to which Drew laughed and said lightheartedly, "That is the perfect sound for the way I feel."

Bronwyn kept walking and muttered to herself, "I just hope it actually changes things."

"You know, I'm actually surprised he's going ahead with this thing. I thought it might be enough for him just to have this privately over me."

Bronwyn nodded, "You're right, it's been so long since the 'incident,' I'm surprised it still matters to him."

"Then again, this is J.D. we're talking about."

"I've never known him to let anything go. He can carry a grudge forever."

They walked on, and Bronwyn realized after it came out that she had turned Drew down, they probably wouldn't get to hang out like this. She would miss him. Not knowing if she would get the chance to anytime soon, she said, "By the way, if I haven't said it, thanks again for doing this for me. For both our sakes, I hope it works."

"If things were different..." Drew drifted off.

"Yeah?"

"Do you think I could just not go along with the terms of the bet? I mean, it's just J.D., I don't really owe him anything."

As desperate as Bronwyn was for a solution that could allow them to be together, she reasoned, "The thing is – the band needs this. You know it does."

The disharmony from band camp had grown and they both knew J.D. needed to 'win' to come back to participating normally with the other sections. Drew admitted, "I really wish Lance was Captain."

"You and me both."

"Drew?" It was Geoff, the brass Captain.

"Yeah?"

"You were going to go over the closer with us?"

"Coming." He looked at Bronwyn and said, "Goodbye."

At the end of 5th period the next day, J.D. held his stick up for attention and addressed the entire Line, "I'd like everyone to be on time tonight. We're going to have a special treat from the drum major before the game."

Tony cracked, "Is this for all of us or just Bronwyn?"

Bronwyn immediately flushed, but she just as quickly flicked Tony off, as many of the members of the Line tried to hold back a laugh.

J.D. winked at Bronwyn and said, "Everyone just be there."

Bronwyn inwardly cringed at J.D.'s leery gesture. As the Line broke attention to put their instruments away, Bronwyn tried to ignore the stares she was getting from the other percussionists. The whole situation was getting too complicated. She knew they all thought *she* knew what was going to happen tonight…which she did know, but wasn't supposed to know. Plus, if a drummer had somehow missed the drum major personally squiring the only girl on the Battery after the past two games, they had certainly heard about it from someone else on the Line. Therefore, Bronwyn was not surprised to hear a purposely loud afterthought from Tony.

"It's just disrespectful if you ask me. I mean, it's like Drew thinks he's better than us because he's drum major or something. And if Bronwyn is with him, well… "

Bronwyn painfully clamped down on the inside of her cheek, knowing exactly what the first bass was insinuating. She had to use every bit of restraint not to yell at her fellow sophomore.

Just remember something nice…

Drew's kiss was nice.

Well, concentrate on that.

A smirking Tony seemed to notice he had almost gotten to the normally unshakable Bronwyn. He asked, "What's the matter, Flueger? Why don't you go ahead and tell everyone what Drew's going to tell us tonight?"

Bronwyn took a deep breath and responded casually, "Sorry, Tony, I hate to disappoint you, but he's not my boyfriend. What do you care anyway? Do *you* have feelings for me or something?"

Tony had kept up a stream of annoying comments since band camp. After seeing Drew with her, he had an entirely new brand of insults to torture her with. However, Tony was clever enough not to torment Bronwyn when senior members of the Line were present. Bronwyn's retort was one of the only times she had ever spoken back to Tony, and those who were in the percussion room paid attention.

"What did you say?"

"I asked why you cared?"

While everyone in the room waited for Tony's response, Lucy's former antagonist, Mark, 'accidentally' bumped Tony's shoulder as he left the room. He threw back a sarcastic, "Excuse me."

Bronwyn smiled at Mark's small vote of confidence in her. Emboldened, she repeated herself, "Why do you care, Tony? Does who I date affect how I play snare?"

"No reason."

Bronwyn gathered her bag and left the room, "That's what I thought."

She knew as soon as she walked out he would probably start talking trash about her and Drew, but it had felt good to finally render Tony speechless.

To: karatechop@state.edu
From: FHHSsnaregrl@FHHS.edu

Lucy…

So, a little after the fact, but I have just two words for you: trampoline and stars. The date was totally amazing. I'm not sure even why I'm telling you this, but as first kisses go, mine with Drew was, well, there really aren't words to describe it. So, yeah, I'm totally bummed because that was it, my only shot and now it's over. Drew and I can't see each other and I know it's really going to hurt when I see him date someone else, which I'm sure will be in a week or so.

Any advice to help this messed up sophomore?

B

To: FHHSsnaregrl@FHHS.edu
From: karatechop@state.edu

B,

Sorry things between you guys had to end like this, and, at this point I'm just going to have to take your word that you two couldn't figure out a way around the devious mind of J.D. Strauss.

(Does sarcasm come across on e-mail?)

Anyway, I know the end of the season seems like an eternity away, but can you make it until then? Maybe you and Drew can start things up in the off-season. I know it's not a lot, but maybe the thought of it can keep you going. You should ask him, who knows?

*Take it from a girl who knows from firsthand experience, it's **REALLY** difficult to be with someone the Line doesn't like. However, I guess you have to decide if he's worth it. If your happiness involves having Drew in your life, then maybe say to hell with J.D. and his followers and just go for it.*

Lucy

P.S. Speaking of first kisses…I just had a nice one of my own on Saturday night. A guy in my apartment complex, Joe.

To: crazyhat@state.edu
From: FHHSdmajor@FHHS.edu

Hey bro,

I can't go to anyone else with this situation I've gotten myself into. Long story short, I think I really like this girl, but due to the politics of marching band, we can't be together.

How do I get myself to stop thinking about her?

D—

To: FHHSdmajor@FHHS.edu
From: crazyhat@state.edu

Drew,

"Politics of marching band?" What the hell does that even mean? You like the girl. Well, if you like her enough you'll find a way to be together. End of story.

There's actually a girl I'm interested in up here. We both went to FHHS, but it seems like we've only discovered each other at college. Long story short, I was a junior when she was a freshman. It's funny, looking back all the times we could've met in high school, but I guess it wasn't meant to be until college. Of course, I guess it's a bit complicated between us as well. She's just coming out of a long relationship. Maybe I'm not the best person to be asking advice from.

I'll be coming home soonish (laundry is totally catching up with me), so maybe we can hang out and talk about this in person.

Lates,

Joe

Drew made his way to the percussion room before the night's game, unhappy with what he was about to do. He walked in and saw the entire Line had gathered. Bronwyn was there, sitting in the back, and kept her eyes on the ground.

The drum major took a deep breath, and announced, "So, I just wanted to let all of you know that for the rest of the season, I will leave you the hell alone. J.D. is your Captain and should I have any issue with anyone on the Line, I will consult him first."

With that, Drew turned around and left the room.

What J.D. (and Bronwyn) had hoped would be a bonding moment for the Line fell completely and totally flat. In reality, no one except J.D. (and maybe Tony, as a loyal J.D. follower) understood what Drew's random confession meant, or cared. As the drummers looked around at each other trying to figure out what the heck had just happened, J.D. burst out laughing.

No one in the room joined in.

Lance looked around and asked skeptically, "What exactly are you laughing at, J.D.?"

"That was priceless."

Jared looked at J.D. and said, "No, it wasn't. That was just weird. I mean, we're not exactly kicking ass and taking names this year. Don't we need to get along with the drum majors?"

Bronwyn breathed out a sigh she didn't realize she was holding in.

J.D. looked around the room, desperate to keep the attention on Drew and how much he didn't like his classmate. After a few moment of struggling for the appropriate response, he said, "Well, Flueger, there's something else you should know. Your precious 'boyfriend' placed a bet on you."

Bronwyn's heart sank. She had to act surprised, which wasn't difficult to do, given J.D.'s confession. "He did what?!"

"Apparently, he was so sure you were going to say yes to going out with him that he made a wager with me."

With all her emotions so close to the surface, it didn't take much for Bronwyn to pretend to be upset. She sputtered, "I don't understand. Why would he do that?"

"I just thought you should see what kind of guy he really is."

Bronwyn stood up and pointed at J.D., "I'll tell you what I do see. I see a Captain who took a bet on someone in his section. I see a section leader who is too busy to care about what really matters. I see…" She stopped, and continued, "Why would you care anyway? No one on this Line gives a shit about me!"

With her heart pounding, Bronwyn roughly grabbed Stewie and her carrier and walked out of the room.

Chapter Nine

Rumors

Silently questioning her sanity, Bronwyn put her drum on the instrument truck and desperately wished she could ride on one of the band buses with the rest of her friends. With her little outburst she was pretty sure no one was going to want to sit with her on the drum line bus. Seeing Megan and Meredith, Bronwyn walked in their direction.

Why did I have to sound like such a girl back there?

Uh, duh? You are one.

But this is drum line, not the dance line…

Quit whining. Maybe this whole time you've been trying to hard to hide the fact that you are a girl. What's so wrong with being a girl? Last time I checked, most guys *like* girls.

Maybe.

Well, standing up to Tony was a good start. You can be a girl, but just because you act like a girl doesn't mean you can't be strong. Remember Lucy?

Desperate to avoid the percussionists, Bronwyn thought about her situation and chatted with her band friends, keeping one eye on the drummers boarding their bus. Not wanting to relive her mistake from a few minutes before, she kept quiet about her little blow up at the Line, and decided to tell her friends at a later date. She purposely got on last and was about to take a seat in the front near the chaperones when someone spoke up from the back.

"Yo, Flueger…back here."

It was Lance. Bronwyn didn't question his motives; she went back and slid into the seat, making sure she was closest to the window. Once the bus got going and everyone had pulled out their Real Feel pads, the sophomore relaxed a little. She wasn't sure how this ride was going to end, but listening to the sounds of the bus, she knew she was somewhere part of her belonged.

Bronwyn looked out the window and wished she had a phone so she could text Drew.

Do you really think he wants to talk to you right now?

Bronwyn tried not to think of the answer to that question and looked around the bus. She was sitting in one of the very back seats, with Jared and Mark across the aisle. J.D. was sitting a few seats further up and out of hearing range. Bronwyn accidentally locked eyes with Tony, who smirked at her. She looked away and slid further down in her seat, trying her best to become invisible. Lance had already pulled out his sticks and was practicing on the back of the seat. Bronwyn wasn't sure why he had called her to sit with him, but whatever the reason, she was grateful. She was about to pull out her iPod and completely cut herself off from the bus, when Lance asked, "So, you don't like J.D. that much, do you?"

She didn't bother keeping her voice down as she replied sarcastically, "What made you think that?"

"So, why not just confront him about it?"

Bronwyn gave him an incredulous look.

"Seriously, I know it's hard to believe, but I think somewhere, deep down he is human."

Bronwyn gave her fellow snare another skeptical look. Although if Lance was willing to admit J.D. had redeeming qualities, maybe she should hear him out. She crossed her arms, and said, "Who cares about J.D.? I haven't noticed you doing anything."

Lance thought a moment and drummed a tough lick on the back of the seat, then commented, "It's different."

"You're right; of course it is."

Bronwyn pulled out her own sticks and began drumming along with Lance. Mark, across the aisle, propped his Real Feel pad on his knees. Lance turned his back to Bronwyn and began drumming with Mark. The typically loquacious pair were unusually quiet as they drummed. Bronwyn wasn't sure if she had said the wrong thing or not.

Suddenly, Mark looked up and asked, "B, were you serious about what you said earlier?"

Bronwyn's blue grey eyes widened, "What if I was?"

"Is that what you really think?"

"Have you guys given me any reason to think otherwise?" Mark and Lance kept drumming. Bronwyn continued, "It's not the same for you guys. You're seniors, so you can pretty much do whatever you want."

Mark grinned, "Or whoever we want!"

The boys clicked their sticks together.

Bronwyn rolled her eyes and asked, "I don't understand. Why does J.D. have such a problem with Drew anyway?"

Lance stopped drumming, "Actually, I have a question. Why do the rest of the sophomores have such a problem with *you*?"

"What does that have to do with anything?!"

From the other side of Mark, Jared asked, "Since when was being on the Line such a big soap opera?"

Mark laughed and answered, "Since our sophomore year!"

The guys all laughed at some inside joke that Bronwyn obviously didn't get. Lance picked up on the confused look on her face, "It was before your time."

Jared said, "Believe it or not, we all used to be in the same section."

Bronwyn vaguely remembered seeing the drum line shirt from a few years ago as well as some of the stories that Lucy had told her. She commented, "You guys must've had a blast."

"We did."

Lance finished a long roll, "Things were different then."

Mark looked across the seats, and said with a cocky smile on his face, "Don't worry too much, B, we'll take care of things."

Feeling overcome with emotion for the fourth time in the past hour, Bronwyn looked away and put on her headphones. Losing herself in familiar tunes, she settled back into her seat. The three seniors had given her a lot to consider.

Why do the rest of the sophomores dislike me so much?

Not one person had stood up for Bronwyn during her outburst. No one in her class had come up to her to see what was going on, if she was okay, or if she needed any help. It was a disturbing fact and one Bronwyn wanted to get to the bottom of.

When the band pulled up to the opposing high school for the evening, Bronwyn was no closer to figuring out what to do about J.D., Drew, or the rest of the Line. She knew the cause of the sophomore class's irritation with her was mostly due to Tony's persistent personality. With nothing particularly great to focus on in the present, she thought ahead. Where did their current relationship get them? Although she was begrudged to admit it, Tony was the next most talented drummer in their class. If they still hated each other by the time they were seniors, what would that mean for their last season? Would they be repeating the same mistakes of J.D. and Lance? Would each practice be a power struggle? Every performance a chance to show up the other? Lance's question really struck a chord with Bronwyn. She thought about her ultimate goal on the Forrest Hills drum line – to be Captain. Bronwyn was almost positive that a girl had never held the position, but knew she could lead the section. However, would she want to manage a group of people who didn't believe in her?

"Let's go, B," Lance said, bringing her attention back to the noisy bus.

As she walked over to collect Stewie from the equipment truck, the snare drummer tried not to notice, but she was getting some weird stares from the rest of the band as they warmed up. She tried a few times to get Drew's attention, but he wouldn't even look up to give her eye contact. Shrugging, she decided it would probably be best to keep her head down and drum her ass off this evening. On the field, Bronwyn was always happy – everything else seemed to disappear as she marched the drill and played the notes.

As was tradition, the third quarter left everyone filling up on caffeine and candy at the concession stands. While digging out some change from her uniform pants, Bronwyn spotted her friends, who proceeded to bodily drag her away from the gathered teenagers.

"What gives, girls?"

Meredith looked curiously at Bronwyn, "So…?"

Bronwyn, oblivious, sipped her drink, "Yes?"

Meredith continued, "Anything you want to tell us?"

"You mean you guys have *already* heard? I thought the news would at least be contained to our bus until maybe next week."

Meredith put her arm around Bronwyn and explained, "It's not your fault. Sandra walked by the percussion room at exactly the wrong time."

Bronwyn groaned. Sandra was the band gossip. She summoned her courage and asked, "How bad is it?"

Megan replied, "I'm not going to lie to you, there were a lot of rumors on our bus."

Bronwyn sighed, "This is *so* not what I need. For your information, Drew simply informed our section that he does not have any control over the Line. That's all. I don't really see what the big deal is or how it affects everyone else."

They were back at the stands. Since the third quarter wasn't quite over, Bronwyn went and sat with her friends in the woodwind section. Meredith looked around and said, "I *wish* that's what Sandra had overheard."

Bronwyn had a sinking feeling in her stomach, "Wait, what exactly did she hear? What has she been telling people?"

Meredith and Megan shared a look.

"Guys, you're scaring me! What does everyone know?"

Megan said slowly, "She overheard the part that Drew made a bet that you would go out with him."

Bronwyn let out a string of expletives she had been overhearing all season. Her friends looked at her as if she had sprouted a second head. When the redhead collected herself, she replied, "Sorry girls, it was either that or start sobbing uncontrollably."

Meredith asked, "What are you going to do about it?"

"I don't know, but I'm sure that this is exactly what J.D. wanted to happen."

The buzzer sounded loudly, ending the third quarter. Bronwyn sighed and got up, "I gotta get back to Stewie. See if you can't help me with damage control during the rest of the night."

Megan asked, "What do you want us to tell people?"

That it wasn't true. That I put Drew up to the whole thing. That I'm the world's biggest idiot...

Instead she instructed, "Just tell everyone that Sandra must've misheard."

Unlike earlier in the evening, Bronwyn was actually grateful to get on the drum line bus to avoid the rumors regarding herself and the senior drum major. Now that the *entire* band thought Drew had "bet" on her and she had turned him down, there was really no way of public reconciliation. His reputation was also totally in question. People were wary of following the direction of some guy who had nothing better to do than bet on whether or not girls would go out with him. Bronwyn had heard what people were saying in the stands and felt terrible. Things were spinning out of control faster than the Guard could twirl their flags.

What's the alternative? If you come clean...

...no one will believe me! There's got to be something to make this situation normal.

Let's hope, because now the ENTIRE band is one dysfunctional mess.

For what seemed like the millionth time since they got on the bus, Bronwyn sighed loudly. How could she not have guessed what J.D. was going to do?

Lance looked over at her strangely and commented, "You've done that way too often on this trip."

Mark looked across the aisle, "Yeah, what's up? I mean I thought we had talked everything through on the way up here."

Jared chimed in, "That's the problem with girls. Way too much talking."

Bronwyn took a deep breath and looked around to see if anyone else on the bus was paying attention. They weren't. She said quietly, "I didn't tell you guys that the bet was my idea."

Mark and Lance exchanged a doubtful look. Lance asked skeptically, "Your idea?"

Bronwyn crossed her arms and said defensively, "Yes, as a matter of fact, it was."

Mark asked suggestively, "Why would Drew go along with it? Did you make him an offer he couldn't refuse?"

Bronwyn sighed and pretended to dig her iPod out.

Mark put up his hands, "Okay, okay, but seriously, Drew looked like an idiot today."

"All part of the plan."

Lance chuckled, "So I'm guessing some part of this magical plan didn't turn out the way you thought it would?"

"Promise not to tell anyone?"

Mark smirked, "What is this? The dance line bus? Yeah, yeah, we won't tell anyone."

"Okay, here's the thing," Bronwyn couldn't believe the words as they rushed out of her mouth, "I saw how everyone was last year with Lucy on the Line. It's never been that way for me. After band camp when Drew and J.D. were all 'we hate each other,' I figured a good way to get everyone to like me would to have me do something heroic in front of J.D. I went to Drew and he actually agreed and then we sort of planted the idea for the bet on J.D. He totally went with it. Are you with me so far?"

Lance and Mark stared at the snare drummer blankly. Bronwyn thought about what she had just finished saying. It didn't really make any sense at all. She shook her head, put her hands over her ears and said, "I'm obviously going insane. Please pretend you didn't hear any of it."

Mark shook his head, "See, maybe that's the thing that made Lucy so cool. She wouldn't have done anything like that."

"Well, that's because everyone in her year actually liked her. It's easier when everyone from your class doesn't totally resent you. Plus, Billy was a much cooler Captain than J.D. will ever be."

Lance asked, "Are you sure that's the reason?"

Jared had been listening in. He commented, "Why didn't you just go to your section in the first place and ask them about it, Bronwyn? I mean it's not like you guys didn't practice all summer together. Some of this has got to be in your head. I mean Lance is right here, why not talk to him?"

Rather than admitting Jared was correct or face whatever harsh truth Lance was going to tell her, Bronwyn ignored the bass player entirely and answered, "So, my own mental capacity aside, somehow, inexplicably, let's pretend everyone is now Team Bronwyn. What do I do about the Drew mess? If J.D. finds out he's been played, then I'm in an even worse position than where I started and if I don't do something to set everyone straight about Drew, then he looks like a complete asshole…which, by the way, he did not sign up for."

Mark asked bluntly, "Why even worry about what the rest of the band thinks about Drew? He went along with your crazy little pact. Let him suffer the consequences."

Bronwyn sighed; she didn't want to let Drew burn for this.

Lance asked, "What if you can convince J.D. that Drew set the whole thing up and you had no idea what was going on?"

Bronwyn rolled her eyes, "What does Drew have to gain from that?"

Jared said, "Yeah, I guess you're screwed."

Mark laughed, "If the truth gets out, J.D. is going to be super pissed."

"You're not helping, Mark."

Lance continued drumming, but remarked, "Personally, even if you told the truth, I doubt he would believe you."

Everyone shared a look. Bronwyn said, "It's highly doubtful."

Sagacious Lance continued, "So, make amends with Drew. Start a new rumor, and put the whole thing behind you."

Bronwyn leaned back in her seat and said, "I'll think about it. Thanks for listening to me tonight guys, I appreciate it."

Chapter Ten

Discussions

Back at Forrest Hills, Bronwyn knew she had to get her snare in the percussion room and out to Drew's car before he left. Given his current reputation, she didn't imagine he wanted to stick around or felt like hanging out with anyone. The bus pulled up and Bronwyn was the first at the equipment truck. She quickly dragged Stewie and stowed her instrument in the percussion room, then sprinted out to Drew's car and waited. The seconds ticked by like minutes. Finally, Bronwyn saw Drew approaching from a distance. She realized she had no idea what she was going to say to him. In the end, that concern would prove to be irrelevant. Drew completely ignored her as he got in his car and drove off. Bronwyn wasn't surprised when the emotions she had been trying to keep in check all evening spilled over. She stood numbly in the dark night.

Drew couldn't help it as he glanced in his rearview mirror at Bronwyn's small and lonely figure fading in the night as he roared away from the school. Clearing the first stoplight, he found his cell phone and immediately dialed his brother. Frustrated, the Forrest Hills drum major heard his brother's voicemail. Drew punched the numbers again, hoping Joe was around to take the call. After a few rings, Joe picked up. Drew didn't even give his older brother a chance to speak, "Dude, I totally need your help!"

For a moment, Drew didn't hear anything on the other end of the phone. Then, straining his ears, he distinctly heard music, a female voice, some muffled laughter, and a door shutting, before his brother responded, "Drew..."

"Did you hear me? I need some help!"

"Fine, but you owe me big, little bro. *Real* big."

Drew did not want to interrupt his brother's love life, but since his own was in a state of complete chaos, he didn't feel like cutting his brother much slack, "Fine."

"So, what's up?"

"Okay, remember the 'political situation' I was telling you about."

"Umm...yeah. I still don't understand how there can be politics in marching band, especially since you're allegedly leading the whole group, but go ahead."

"Anyway—"

"Hey Drew?" His brother interrupted.

"Yes?"

"I have a, uh, friend here who was in marching band, maybe she can help you out."

"She...?" Despite how angry Drew was at the world, he had a definite interest in any 'she' that was in his brother's life.

"Yeah, maybe you knew her."

"What's her name?"

"Lucy—"

"Karate?"

"Yeah, you know her? She's a very cool chick."

Drew sighed – of course he knew Lucy Karate. Everyone in the Forrest Hills HS Marching Band knew of the flirtatious, cute brunette who just so happened to play a mean bass drum. He was also fairly certain that Lucy and Bronwyn were still in touch.

Maybe she can help?

Maybe she'll go right to Bronwyn and tell her everything.

I say you give her a chance. If she's good enough for Joe...

"Okay, put her on."

While Joe went in search of Lucy, Drew thought about the former drum line sweetheart. Even though Drew had been drum major the previous year, he hadn't interacted that much with the Line. He never got to know the bass drummer because his co-drum major, Fred, had been tight with both Lucy and Billy. Anything that came up with the section had been Fred's territory. Drew hadn't exactly felt left out, but he never really had a chance to get to know anyone in the Line except the Pit – which was exactly where this situation had started.

"Drew?" A female voice came over the line.

"Yup?"

"So, what's this about band politics?"

Drew suddenly hesitated, "Well, I don't know if you're the best person to talk to."

"Uh, dude, I kind of wrote the book on band politics. Remember? Your sophomore year?"

Drew thought a moment and then remembered the controversy of Lucy's romantic interest with the rival school's drum line Captain, not to mention some of the rumors that had swirled around the school during her senior season. He said slowly, "Oh yeah…"

"So, what can I help you with?"

"I still don't know if you're the best person to talk to."

"Because Bronwyn's my friend?"

"Something like that." Drew began to wonder if he had made the right decision by calling his brother.

"Drew, Drew, Drew. I've been around guys long enough to know when to talk and when to keep my mouth firmly closed. So, if you want to talk, that's cool. It's just between us."

The senior paused, before he asked abruptly, "So, you probably know about the 'bet' I had with J.D.?"

"I do."

"Well, plans backfired. Not only did the Line not respond at all to my 'apology,' but the band gossip managed to overhear when J.D. decided to share with everyone that I had bet on Bronwyn going out with me."

"So now you look like a total dick?"

"Basically, yeah."

"And Bronwyn, what does she think?"

"I haven't talked to her about it."

Lucy remarked to herself, "I'll bet she's crushed."

Drew chose to ignore the comment, and tried to forget leaving Bronwyn alone in the parking lot a few minutes earlier, "Anyway, I have lost all credibility with the band."

"Because of a silly bet? Have things changed that much since I graduated?"

"No, but I don't want the rest of my senior year to suck."

"Hmmm."

"Aren't you going to help me?"

Lucy was quiet a moment, then responded, "I guess there's only a few options. Option A, Bronwyn takes all the blame and tells everyone in some manifesto how she arranged the whole thing by herself."

"No one will believe that."

"You are correct, sir. Option B, she tells everyone the truth, that you two were in cahoots and you set up Captain J.D."

"Then J.D. looks like an idiot, and probably will deny everything because that's the kind of guy he is."

"Very true. Which brings us to Option C, you don't do anything and somehow everyone manages to forget what happened."

"Will they?"

"Drew, you're a cute guy—" Lucy paused before saying, "Ouch!"

"I'm a cute guy, ouch? What does that mean?"

"I'm talking to your brother." She continued, half speaking to Joe, "Hey now, cuteness can run in the family. Anyway, before I was so rudely interrupted, I was saying that you're a cute guy and I'm sure the girls in the band will respond to your enhanced 'bad boy' image. As for your leadership, well, just act the part and I'm sure the rest will fall in line."

"You really think so?"

"I think it's pretty much your only option, unless you just want to leave Bronwyn high and dry."

Drew thought a moment, "I don't want to do that."

"Well, I think you should talk to her. I mean, you can't just ignore her."

"I can't?"

"Boys! Here, talk to your brother," Lucy answered, obviously exasperated.

Drew heard the phone being passed back to Joe.

"Bro – you okay now?"

"I think I am."

"Well, I'll see you soon. I think Mom and Dad have forgotten what I look like."

As they said their goodbyes, Drew thought about what he would have to do next.

In the quiet parking lot, Bronwyn wiped her eyes on her hoodie and walked back toward the school. A voice called out, "You need a ride home, B?"

She recognized Ben, and shouted back in what she hoped was he most cheerful voice, "That would be great, thanks."

She walked over to his truck and hopped in, determined not to mention anything about Drew.

Ben had other plans, "So, what a weird night, huh?"

Bronwyn tried her best to feign ignorance and tapped nervously on her knee, "Yeah, I guess."

Ben dropped his voice, "How're you holding up?"

"I—"

"I can't believe Drew actually made a bet on you. I mean, I don't know a lot about him, but that really doesn't sound like anything he would do."

Bronwyn, who felt the evening had been discussed ad nauseum with Jared, Mark, and Lance, said, "I'd really rather not talk about it."

Fortunately, Ben felt his obligation to his passenger's feelings were over, and changed the subject, talking about the game and their performance instead. As they neared Bronwyn's house, the tenor player turned down the radio and asked awkwardly, "So, you sure you're okay? I mean, I don't know a lot about chicks, but tonight couldn't have been that easy."

"Which part could you be referring to? The part where the guy I thought I liked actually bet on me with my Captain? Or the part where the entire band found out about it? I know, how about the part just a few minutes ago where that same guy completely acted like I didn't exist?"

Ben opened his mouth, then closed it again.

Bronwyn continued, "I'm sorry, it's just been a hell of a week...hell of a season so far. I completely understand if you don't ever want to be in a car with me again."

Ben chuckled and stopped the car at Bronwyn's driveway, "Nah, it's not that bad, B. And remember, if you're really feeling bad, I'm sure there are a few people who wouldn't mind trading places with you."

"Really? Name one."

"Only sophomore on snare? Plus, don't forget, you're marching on one of the best Lines in the country. Who really cares if some guy doesn't like you?"

Bronwyn smiled briefly, then collected her things and before she closed the door, said, "Thanks – I really needed to hear that."

Drew thought about what had happened in the parking lot and what Lucy had said.

Maybe you should go over and apologize...

Maybe that's not a bad idea.

Although Drew was almost home, he turned his car around and went directly to Bronwyn's house, hoping to somehow catch her. Pulling into her neighborhood, he saw a vaguely familiar car drive out. The driver was definitely a teenage guy. Drew put the timing together in his head, and assumed whoever the kid in the red truck was had driven Bronwyn home.

It's not like you gave her a lot of options. You left her alone in the parking lot. Can you really blame her?

Drew didn't know who to blame anymore. He got out his phone to call Joe again, but opted for sending a text instead.

>> *Maybe instead of u coming home, I should come up there. Here sux.*

The senior waited for a response, but wasn't surprised when he didn't get one. It wasn't until the following morning when Drew checked his e-mail that his brother decided to answer him.

To: FHHSdmajor@FHHS.edu
From: crazyhat@state.edu

Dude, you need to get laid or something. You're stressing out entirely too much for your senior year. I think you need to do whatever it takes to get over this chick (or politics or whatever has made you Captain Weirdo this semester). If that means coming up here for a weekend, I guess that's cool. If you don't have any competitions, I think I have a free weekend coming up in October.

Lates,

Joe

Ben's words went a long way with the sophomore and Bronwyn managed to think about her disastrous Friday night only once an hour over the weekend. Under the false pretenses of looking for a Homecoming dress, she headed to the mall with Megan and Meredith. While they were taking a break in the Food Court, Bronwyn filled them in on Drew's strange behavior in the parking lot.

Megan munched on a fry and asked, "Well, what did you expect him to do?"

"I don't know. I just wish I could go back in time and never have asked him to help."

Megan laughed, "Yeah, but then you would've never gotten to kiss him."

Megan and Meredith made loud smooching noises, while Bronwyn turned beet red. Meredith finished laughing, then said casually, "So…I have a question."

Bronwyn smiled, glad the subject had changed, and said, "What's up?"

"How well do you know Ben?"

Bronwyn looked quizzically at her friend and mentally sized up the potential pair. She could definitely see her sometime chauffeur and her favorite flute player happily dating. Plus, just because her recent foray into romance was a colossal defeat, it didn't mean other people had to miss out. She replied, "Enough to know you guys would totally be a cute couple."

Meredith grinned, "So, you'll help?"

Bronwyn nodded, "I'll put in a good word."

To: karatechop@state.edu
From: FHHSsnaregrl@FHHS.edu

Lucy,

Ready for the understatement of the year? Things didn't turn out exactly how I thought they would. Drew went through with his part of the deal, but after he left, and there was no response, J.D. decided to tell everyone that Drew had made a bet on me. No big deal for the Line, but of course, at that moment Sandra walked by and heard everything and by the end of the 3rd quarter, everyone in the entire band knew what happened.

To top things off, I tried to go and talk to Drew, but he completely ignored me.

However, it's not all bad. I guess some of the guys on the Line like me a little better. I can't tell if it's a reaction to a little hissy fit I threw or because maybe they just actually like me. Who knows? Boys are weird.

B

P.S. Maybe I can convince my parents about coming up to visit you so I get away from all this chaos.

Chapter Eleven

How Do You Talk To A Drummer?

Bronwyn walked into fifth period on Monday as if nothing had happened. She crossed her fingers, hoping not a word would be mentioned about Friday night's drama. She watched Tony walking over to her with a big grin on his face, and knew she would not be so lucky.

"Hey Bronwyn…"

Bronwyn ignored Tony and walked into the percussion room and began pulling out Stewie.

"How was your weekend?" Tony was nothing, if not persistent.

Bronwyn rolled her eyes, but replied extra sweetly, "It was fine, thanks for asking. How was yours?"

"Whatever."

Bronwyn got out her snare stand and went to set up in the half arc. The first bass player, who was not one to give up easily, continued following her. He asked casually, "So, I guess if you turned Drew down, then you really don't care too much about him?"

"It would appear I don't. I turned him down," Bronwyn commented lightly.

"If you don't like him, I guess it wouldn't matter that I saw your oh-so-dreamy drum major and the Guard Captain at the movies on Saturday night?"

"I-I—"

"That's what I thought."

Jared yelled from across the room, "Hey Tony – you want to think about getting your drum out?"

Tony smirked and went to the percussion room. Bronwyn was beyond embarrassed and completely surprised at the tears welling up in her eyes. She forced her turbulent emotions down and numbly went through warm ups. Her thoughts drifted.

Didn't he feel anything real with me?

Apparently not.

But that night…

Apparently it wasn't the real Drew. Look what he's done since then, ignored you and started dating someone else. Does he really deserve any further thought?

"Flueger?" J.D. snarled and got her attention. It was then she realized she was the only person still playing.

"Sorry."

Her Captain gave her a stern look and then said, "Let's start with the closer."

To: FHHSsnaregrl@FHHS.edu
From: karatechop@state.edu

B,

Sorry to hear things didn't go according to plan…but sometimes life just works out differently than we want it to. Did Wes and I plan to stay together even though we are living thousands of miles apart? Yes. Did I know I was going to meet someone new? No. Okay, sorry to digress from your problems, but I'm kind of a weird place here and trying to sort things out.

So, hopefully, you can just put your drum on and put all this behind you. Chalk it up to a life lesson and move forward. Who knows? Sometimes the guy and girl do get together in the end. Keep your fingers crossed, keep playing a clean show, and I'm sure everything will turn out okay.

Luce

P.S. I think I mentioned I have fall break in late October. Maybe you can come up then? It would be great to see you – and I still need to get back to Forrest Hills to see you march a game!

Bronwyn woke up the following morning completely unmotivated. Usually she looked forward to any day she got to wear her drum, and especially days when she got to see Drew, but today she felt anything but excited. To make things worse, she had spent most of the previous evening looking through her freshman yearbook scanning for pictures of Christina, the Guard Captain. It seemed Christina was everything Bronwyn was not. Christina was a beautiful brunette with stunning locks like a Pantene commercial, long legs and was an amazingly talented dancer. She had been on the Homecoming court for the junior class last year. Even though she knew she didn't have a future with

Drew, seeing her 'competition' had definitely not made Bronwyn feel any better. She had called Megan and Meredith to see if they could confirm Tony's rumor, which, unfortunately they could. No less than five members of the Flyers marching band had seen the duo together. Reports ranged from "cute couple" to "just friends."

Fortunately, the educational portion of her day passed quickly and before long Bronwyn was grabbing Stewie to head down to the practice field. The sophomore was pleasantly surprised when Ben decided to join her. They both walked while leaning back to relieve some of the pressure of the weight of their drums.

Bronwyn said, "I wonder if I'll ever go back to walking normally."

"Not likely."

Bronwyn looked over at Ben's seemingly massive tenor drums, which she had never really worn before and asked, "Want to switch?"

Knowing most people had a weird obsession with 'trying on' other instruments, Ben shrugged and took off his quints. Usually instrument switching only went on in the stands, but if anyone wanted to carry the heavy tenors down to the field, he was all for it. The sophomore almost collapsed when she put on the weighty quints.

"How do you carry these things?!"

"Why am I not playing snare?" Ben said at the same time.

They looked at each other and laughed. Ben looked normal with the snare, but the quints looked ridiculous on Bronwyn's petite frame.

"Want to switch back?"

Bronwyn shook her head, "Nah, it'll make me appreciate Stewie that much more when I get him back."

"You named your drum?"

"Uh, yes. Doesn't everyone?"

"Uh, no."

Wanting to change the topic, Bronwyn asked, "So, Ben?"

"Yeah?"

Bronwyn wasn't exactly sure how to proceed next. She had Ben's attention and by now it was pretty easy to talk to him. With nothing to lose and everything to gain, she queried, "Are you seeing anyone right now?"

Ben looked at her weirdly, "Not really, why?"

She stated hesitantly, "Umm, I know someone that likes you."

"Really?"

"Yeah, do you know my friend Meredith?"

Ben hesitated a moment before saying, "On flute?"

Bronwyn knew the pause was intentional. He *had* noticed her friend. She nudged him, "So you *do* know her?"

Ben tried not to look embarrassed, "I'm glad we're talking about Meredith. For a minute there, I thought you were talking about yourself."

Something about that statement struck Bronwyn as the funniest thing she had ever heard. She burst into hysterical laughter while other band members looked at her strangely.

Drew looked up to see classmates coming down to practice. He wished he had not chosen that exact moment to look up. Seeing Bronwyn flirt with that guy on quints irritated him on a level he didn't think was possible.

What is she wearing?

Those would be quints my friend, *Ben's* quints.

Did the other night mean nothing to her?

Hearing Bronwyn's happy laughter peal across the parking lot caused him to grimace. He felt himself clenching a fist, which was very weird considering he classified himself as a non-violent person. He was still staring at the pair when he felt someone at his side.

"Hey there, handsome." Christina smiled at him.

Drew looked over at the beautiful brunette next to him and felt a flash of guilt. The only reason he had called her over the weekend was that he knew she had a long running crush on him and probably wouldn't care about his current reputation. The senior tried to force thoughts of the redheaded snare out of his head.

"Hey yourself," Drew finally responded.

He could tell Christina was probably wondering if he was going to ask her out again, and Drew really wasn't sure what the answer to that question was. They had shared a nice evening together on Saturday, but it lacked the magic that his trampoline date with Bronwyn had. Drew's blue eyes flicked to the far side of the field where Bronwyn was still (!) talking to Ben.

Obviously she didn't waste any time…

He asked Christina, "Do you want to go out after the game on Friday?"

A blush broke out over her pretty features and she answered, "I'd love to."

"Great, I'll talk to you at practice on Thursday."

"Sounds great. I'll talk to you soon."

Drew watched as she walked away, doubt filling his mind.

Obviously he didn't waste any time…

Bronwyn's eyes narrowed on the female figure leaving Drew's side. On the inside, a small part of her was dying, but she was determined to continue talking normally with Ben. She forced her gaze from Drew, and returned her attention to the quint player, "So, you want me to talk to her?"

Ben rolled his eyes, "Hello, B, this is not 4th grade. I am perfectly capable of talking to a girl by myself."

"Understood." Bronwyn looked to see the rest of the Line pretty much assembled, "Looks like we'd better get into formation."

Due to the odd 'truce' between J.D. and Drew, the band actually made progress during practice that day. Although they were still behind for the season, the show was starting to really come together. Everyone in the band seemed committed to making their performance the best it could be. During the last water break, an impromptu game of Keep-Away with a broken tenor head had started on the far side of the field, involving the Sousa and trumpet players versus the members of the Line.

"Ouch! Damn it!"

Even from across the field, it was obvious someone in pain. Listening to the stream of curse words that followed, it sounded like someone was in excruciating pain. Bronwyn thought she recognized the voice. Rushing over, she was saddened to see Kevin holding his wrist in agony. Bronwyn's heart sank; not only was he an all around nice guy, he was also a strong member of the snare line.

J.D. was already at his side, "Are you okay?"

Kevin's face was white with pain. He shook his head and answered grimly, "No."

One of the band parents came over and cleared the scene, "C'mon guys, I'm a nurse. Let me get a look at that arm."

She poked and prodded things for a minute before making a decision; "I can't tell if it's a break or a sprain, but either way, we'll need to get you to the ER."

Henry immediately volunteered, "I'll take him."

Bronwyn shared a look with the rest of the snares and then unconsciously felt her own arms. She couldn't imagine an injury like that; there was no way she'd be able to play if her arm was in a cast. A bad sprain might go away, but if it was broken...

The band did a run through of the full show a few times, but the Line was obviously distracted. After practice, they lingered in the percussion room. J.D. looked around at his section and said, "I'm sure we're all concerned about Kevin at the moment. I'll try and get information from him tonight and we'll discuss things tomorrow during class."

Silently, the percussionists cleared the room. Ben and Bronwyn walked out to the car. As soon as Ben closed the door, she asked, "What happens next?"

"I have no idea. I mean, if it's a sprain then I'm sure his doctor won't let him march for a week or two."

"Has there ever been an injury like this on the Line?"

Ben thought a moment, then answered, "Nah, well, I mean my freshman year, our Captain, Jerm somehow managed to do something weird to his eye. Anyway, it didn't compromise his playing…he just looked like a modern day pirate."

"Do you think Henry would replace Kevin?"

Ben tapped a finger on his chin, "You know, if it was any other section, maybe, but there's already five of you who have the same part, so why would he need another?"

"Yeah, well, I think Henry wouldn't care, but somehow I think J.D. will be pissy about only marching five snares."

"True. I guess we'll have to wait until tomorrow to find out."

Bronwyn nodded, "I hope Kevin's okay."

Everyone hurried through lunch the next day and assembled before the final bell had rung. Bronwyn pulled out Stewie and was looking down the snare line to see if Kevin was taking his place. He wasn't. He was, however, sitting near the Pit and his left hand was in a cast. The sophomore looked down at her own left hand. It was so pivotal for playing traditional grip. She shuddered and was reminded of how lucky she was to play each and every day. The crisp notes of a snare drum brought her true happiness and she couldn't imagine her life without music.

With a nod from J.D., Kevin stood up and tried his best to keep a smile on his face, "Well, the bad news is, I broke my wrist. The good news is we won the game yesterday!"

His attempt at humor fell flat. No one wanted to see a member of the Line out of commission. J.D. stepped forward and addressed the group, "Now, I've spoken with Kevin and he is in favor of what I'm about to say. I'd like to hold auditions for Kevin's spot on the snare line."

There were exclamations from everyone. It was unheard of to replace someone this far into the season.

Lance asked, "Are you sure that's really necessary? I mean, everyone already has assigned parts. If we take someone away from their original section, won't the rest of the Line suffer?"

J.D. responded, "Look, there's no way I'm going to go into Indoor with any less than six snares!"

Arms crossed, Jared questioned, "So, as long as the snares are fine, it doesn't matter about the rest of us?"

The other sections nodded in agreement.

J.D. glared at the drummers, before he admitted, "Fine. We'll hold auditions and only if we feel someone is really worth it, will they be bumped up to snare."

Bronwyn asked curiously, "How are we going to deem who is good enough to be on snare? And who's judging, you? Henry? The rest of *your* section?"

Mark responded, "Seriously. I mean you can't expect the section leaders to audition – they are needed where they are."

J.D. shook his head, "Listen, I'm the Captain, so show a little respect. Consider the audition piece the snare break during the drum solo. If anyone can do that, they deserve to be in the section."

The rest of the snares shared a look and nodded; it was obvious they didn't think anyone would be able to pull off the very difficult solo Henry had written.

Lance asked, "You sure you don't want to run this past Henry? I bet he might have a problem with your little plan."

"Before I was so rudely interrupted, I was also going to tell everyone that I called Henry last night. There's been some sort of family emergency and he will be out of town for at least a week. He told me to handle things the way I saw fit. This is the way I see them. Auditions are during class on Monday. Consider yourselves warned."

Bronwyn idly wondered if anyone would actually audition. The snares had been working through the difficult solo for weeks to get it clean.

Chapter Twelve

Drum Line Idol

During sectionals on Wednesday afternoon, things in the snare line were very tense. With one-sixth of the section missing, Bronwyn couldn't explain it, but suddenly the group seemed a lot smaller. Finishing off a break, J.D. signaled the group to stop. Lance asked casually, "So, just who exactly were you planning on having judge this 'audition' on Monday?"

J.D. clicked his sticks together and said nonchalantly, "Well, me, I guess."

Bronwyn and Lance shared an exasperated look, before Bronwyn asked, "Really? Just you?"

Even Adam and Scott looked skeptical.

J.D. half-smiled as he answered, "Just kidding. We'll all have an equal say and for someone to get the position they will have to get four of us to say yes."

Lance asked, "Does that include Kevin?"

J.D. replied, "Yes. Kevin will be included. So, a potential candidate has to have four of the six of us give them a thumbs up. We'll do it by blind vote, so none of our 'auditonees' can be crappy about it later. Does everyone agree?"

Hearing murmurs of 'yes' and 'this is worse than electing the Pope,' Bronwyn sighed, relieved that J.D. hadn't gone completely psycho and was actually including the rest of his section in the process. She had briefly debated going to Mr. Izzo with J.D.'s crazy plan, but rationalized that there was a very slim chance that a) someone would nail the solo and b) all the snares would agree on that person.

Scott asked, "Do you think anyone actually has the guts to try out?"

J.D. shrugged and said, "I don't know, but let it be understood that none of us can offer any additional help. If someone comes to you for advice, just tell them you're being diplomatic and can't."

The snares all nodded. It was probably the first time all season they had all been in agreement on something.

76

There was a lot of buzz surrounding the Forrest Hills percussion section by Thursday's practice. The word had gotten out throughout the marching band that the Line was looking for a replacement snare drummer. At the first water break, Bronwyn was surprised when a nervous Pete asked her, "So, can anyone try out?"

"I don't know. Why are you asking?"

"Well, I mean you can't just limit the audition to members of the Line. Maybe there are other drummers out there."

Bronwyn thought a moment before diplomatically answering, "If anyone in this band can cleanly play the solo from the snare break, they will get the spot, no matter which section they are from."

Tyler, who joined them, asked, "What about the rest of the school? Shouldn't you make everyone aware?"

Bronwyn looked at the pair skeptically before she replied drily, "I'll be sure to bring it to J.D.'s attention."

As she headed back over to her section and got into formation, she whispered to Adam, "Is everyone in the band acting crazy or is it just me?"

Adam stifled a laugh, "Tell me about it. How many wannabe snares can there be at Forrest Hills?"

Lance joked from the other side of J.D., "Have they even picked up sticks before? It's not as easy as we make it look."

J.D. looked down the snare line and said, "Alright guys, due to the overwhelming response for Kevin's spot, we're going to have to move the auditions to after school on Monday. I'm going to limit 'non Line' auditions to no more than twenty people. I mean seriously, everyone knows that tryouts are in the spring, if you waited until now, get over it!"

With the excuse of being a member of the judging committee, Bronwyn decided she would actually pay attention to what she was wearing on Monday. While she usually didn't bother too much with her clothing selections, she decided the guys needed a reminder that she was female. Sure, maybe it was for the attention – but what was the point of being in an all guy section if you couldn't get some extra interest now and then? She tried to convince herself that her eye-catching ensemble had nothing to do with constantly seeing a disgustingly happy Drew and Christina at practice. After discussing her options with Megan and Meredith, Bronwyn went out of her usual comfort zone and wore a slim black pencil skirt with a tight green shirt and completed the look with a pair of awesome heels she borrowed from Megan. She even managed to get her crazy red curls under control. Looking at herself in the mirror, Bronwyn was convinced she looked at least sixteen or seventeen and all business.

*Just see if they don't take **my** opinion seriously today.*

Walking into the band room, Bronwyn was pleased to see that her mini-makeover was being noticed. As she walked up to her friends, she could've sworn she saw Pete tuck a pair of drum sticks into his book bag, but decided against it, guessing it must've been something else instead.

After school, Bronwyn and Kevin watched as the guys set up the band room for auditions. Bronwyn looked at the senior's cast and asked, "Mind if I sign it?"

"Not at all."

He dug around in his backpack for a Sharpie. Concentrating, Bronwyn marked out a few notes from the snare solo on his cast, "There you go!"

Kevin looked and smiled, "Thanks."

J.D., who was busy moving chairs, looked over at the pair and said, "If you two are done not helping, I think we are ready to begin. Bronwyn, do you want to be our door girl?"

Maybe it was the clothes, or maybe it as the fact that she wanted to blame her failed relationship on her Captain and his big mouth, Bronwyn raised an eyebrow and shot J.D. an ice cold stare; "What did you ask me?"

J.D. tried to backpedal and looked to Kevin for help. Kevin shrugged his shoulders and said, "You're on your own, man."

J.D. put his hands up, "I just meant…well, you look nice today."

Bronwyn crossed her arms, "Any other reason?"

"Seniority?"

"So, because I'm the only sophomore I have to 'fetch' people?"

"Listen, do you want to or not?"

Bronwyn considered her options: on the one hand, it was sort of demeaning work, on the other it was a way to a) possibly get on J.D.'s good side, which, whether she would admit it or not was something she needed to do b) answer the door in Tony's face thereby reminding him again that *she* was on the snare line and he was not and c) potentially meet a cute mystery percussionist who might try out for the Line.

Grudgingly she answered, "Fine, but I'm not getting anyone's coffee."

"Well, go ahead, we're ready for the first 'contestant.'"

Bronwyn looked back at her section, which had assembled at a long table in front of J.D.'s snare. Adam flashed her a thumbs up. She walked to the hallway, and looked at the line of wannabe drummers waiting patiently. Wanting to make them sweat a moment longer, she reviewed the sign up list posted next to the band room door. The simple sheet of paper had two categories, one for current members of the Line, and those who were not. She perused the list again, and paused. Peter Overton.

*Pete? What is **he** doing auditioning?*

Bronwyn continued scanning the list and was surprised to see a girl's name on it. The thought hadn't even occurred to her that another girl would audition. She had already talked to Valerie and Beth and they were both happy continuing to learn the ropes in the Pit. Bronwyn would've considered giving them extra help if she really thought they had a chance. She was surprised when a small part of her was relieved that they weren't going to audition. As much as she didn't want to admit it, even after all of the drama, there was something very fun about being the only girl on the Battery.

She looked at the girl's name again. Dana Berman. It sounded familiar.

I guess I'll see when she shows up.

Bronwyn called the first name and the auditions began. Time went by quickly and before long, the redhead found herself face to face with Tony.

He had his trademark smirk already in place, "I guess I can't count on your vote, can I, Flueger?"

Bronwyn resisted the urge to stick out her tongue, and instead replied, "Unlike you, Tony, I have something called integrity. I'm actually going to wait and see if you can play."

"Whatever."

"And, by the way, I'm sure the rest of the basses are *so* proud of you."

Bronwyn smiled smugly and took her seat next to Adam.

J.D. said, "Tony, either you know the piece or you don't. Just play it."

As much as Bronwyn was hoping he would crash and burn, Tony did a pretty solid job of really knocking out the solo. When he had finished, everyone sat quietly. J.D. said, "Well, Tony we'll let you know the results tomorrow."

Tony oddly saluted the snare line and walked out of the room.

Lance whistled, "That was weird."

Adam agreed, "I guess he's been practicing."

J.D. said, "Well, let's take a vote."

Everyone wrote on a piece of paper, which J.D. quickly collected and tallied. Unlike the other auditions, this one was unanimous the other way. All six members of the snare line had said "yes" to Tony.

Bronwyn suggested, "Well, maybe now we should look for a replacement for Tony, rather than a replacement for Kevin. We have to at least see everyone else."

Lance agreed, "It's not that bad an idea. I mean, if we can find someone independent and teach them the show quickly, things might work out for everyone."

The theory of trying to find another good player wasn't proving to be very easy. The group was about to give up when Pete showed up at the door.

Bronwyn looked at him skeptically, "What are you doing here?"

Pete puffed himself up, "Auditioning."

"You know, if you had asked, I could've helped you."

Her friend paused at the door and replied, "Um, you seemed a little preoccupied recently."

"Really?"

They walked into the band room and Pete quipped, "Plus, B, don't take this the wrong way, but you're kind of totally intimidating as a drummer."

"Good luck," Bronwyn gave him a smile and joined the seated snares.

Pete wasn't a natural, but he had decent chops. He was definitely the next strongest player after Tony's audition.

J.D. dismissed him by saying, "We'll let you know tomorrow."

Pete said, "Thanks, guys."

As soon as he closed the door, Lance said, "Bass."

J.D. crossed his arms, "Really?"

Adam said, "We're going to need a replacement for Tony. Why shouldn't it be this guy?"

Bronwyn looked at her section, "Hello? Major *problemo?*"

The guys looked at her, before Bronwyn continued, "Pete plays trumpet. Don't you think that Geoff is going to have a problem?"

They all continued looking at her as if she had sprouted another head. J.D. asked, "Who is Geoff?"

Bronwyn knew who Geoff was, because unlike the rest of the girls in band, she had to search for cute guys *outside* her section. She informed the other snares, "Geoff is the Brass Captain."

And totally adorable, she added to herself, before she continued, "He isn't going to like someone in his section just 'switching' out. Imagine if someone on the Line moved themselves to Brass."

As expected, J.D. said, "Well, he can get over it, because if Pete wants the spot, it's his."

Adam asked, "Also, what about his schedule? I mean how is the bass line going to practice every day in class missing the first bass?"

Everyone sighed.

Bronwyn stated, "I happen to know that Pete has Electronic Music Techniques during 5th period."

J.D. smiled and said, "Which is taught by Mr. Walker and we know he won't care. So, there we are, problem solved."

Bronwyn sighed, "Well, we have one more audition."

She walked to the door and remembered exactly who Dana Berman was. Dana was also in marching band, a member of the Guard. Bronwyn tried to clear predetermined judgments from her mind. After all, she would be the worst kind of hypocrite if she didn't give Dana chance. Bronwyn knew how many times people looked at her and assumed she was something other than a great percussionist. She forced a smile on her face and said brightly, "Ready?"

Dana played a below average audition. She also played matched grip, which definitely wouldn't work in the current snare line. She wasn't the worst drummer of the day, but she wasn't as good as Tony or Pete. What she did excel at however, was wardrobe selection. Bronwyn couldn't even remember what she wore for her audition in the spring, but had a feeling that Dana had planned out this outfit carefully. Her classmate was wearing a tight denim miniskirt with an equally tight pink top that didn't leave much to the imagination.

J.D said with a wink, "I'll personally let you know the results tomorrow."

As soon as she shut the door, the guys started making a number of inappropriate comments, gestures, and sounds. Bronwyn was furious. She knew they were kidding, but their reaction was a bit ridiculous. She jumped out of her seat and said coldly, "Seriously?! Are you kidding me?"

The guys were instantly quiet.

Exasperated at their responses, Bronwyn continued, "I know you guys are the most sexually frustrated group in the history of the world, but we are not having someone on this Line because she looks good in a skirt!"

J.D. said quietly, "I'll talk to Tony, Pete, and Izzo tomorrow before practice. Tony can start as a snare as soon as Pete transfers into the class. I will personally work with Tony to catch him up to the part. So, until further notice, sectionals are cancelled."

Chapter Thirteen

This Means War!

Bronwyn went home from auditions with a number of confused feelings. She supposed she should've been glad Pete was now on the Line with her.

Let's face it – you definitely could use more people on Team Bronwyn.

But the Line, that's *my* thing.

Don't feel like sharing, huh?

Not exactly.

It might not have meant a lot to anyone else, but the Line was Bronwyn's. Even in middle school when everyone was just learning their instruments, being a percussionist was what Bronwyn was known for. It's not that she didn't like Pete, but now all the inside jokes and stupid things that went on weren't going to be just hers. Also, since Pete didn't know anyone else really on the Line, she knew it was going to be up to her to look after him for the rest of the season.

Knowing she had a paper due in English, Bronwyn quickly typed an e-mail to Lucy.

To: karatechop@state.edu
From: FHHSsnaregrl@FHHS.edu

Lucy,

*Could this year get any weirder? To catch you up on what has happened over the past week – Kevin broke his wrist, then J.D. held auditions, and bada bing bada boom, my friend Pete (of the trumpet persuasion) is now an official member of the Line. Even worse, **Tony** is now on the SNARE line.*

Also, to answer your earlier question, nothing went anywhere with Drew. I totally underestimated what kind of guy he really is. No sooner does everything happen with us than he's already dating Christina, the perfect Captain of the Guard. They make such a disgustingly gorgeous couple I want to throw up every time I see them. I'm just glad they're both seniors and I will never have to see any of them after marching season!

B

To: FHHSsnaregrl@FHHS.edu
From: karatechop@state.edu

B,

J.D. held auditions? Something about that doesn't seem right at all… What is going on in the Forrest Hills drum line? Where was Henry in all of this?

Furthermore, Drew sounds like a totally different person than how you originally described him / how I remember him. Now, did you ever actually TALK to him about what happened? Because from what you're telling me, it sounds like the answer to that is a big fat NO. I think maybe you'd be surprised if you just actually sat down with him. Hasn't enough time passed where you two can speak normally to each other?

L

To: karatechop@state.edu
From: FHHSsnaregrl@FHHS.edu

Luce,

What would there be to talk about? He made it perfectly clear the night in the parking lot when he COMPLETELY IGNORED ME. He should just go and be happy with her and go have a perfect time at Homecoming and I'll just worry about marching a clean season.

Can I come up for your Fall Break weekend? Please… I'm pretty close to desperate here. I think a change of scenery would do me a lot of good. Do you think my parents would notice if I transferred to State?

B

To: FHHSsnaregrl@FHHS.edu
From: karatechop@state.edu

B,

Of course you can come up. See if you can score a ride from anyone and just bring a sleeping bag and plan on banishing ALL negative thoughts while you're here. Pam does not allow them!

Although, full disclosure, remember that guy in my apartment complex I was telling you about? Well, that guy is actually Joe, who is actually Drew's older brother … !!! What tangled webs we weave, huh? I didn't think it was serious, but I officially ended things with Wes recently and well, who knows where this relationship will go?

I should also mention that Drew called me that night (well, he really called Joe, but we ended up talking for awhile). And even though I know you won't want to, you might want to give the kid a break, he seemed pretty confused. I don't know if that's worth anything to you now, but deep down I think well, you should ask him yourself. If you don't think it's too late, there might be something salvageable in your crazy season.

Luce

Bronwyn slowly digested the information from Lucy's most recent e-mail. She needed to know more than electronic words were going to provide. Without hesitation, she called her friend.

Lucy answered on the second ring, "I was wondering if you would call."

"Why didn't you tell me?"

The college freshman paused a moment before she replied, "Well, Drew neglected to mention the whole leaving you standing alone part, so I wasn't really getting the entire story."

"Still…"

"In my defense, Drew was calling his brother, and didn't realize I was going to be there. It was a fine line of whose confidence I would be betraying. Plus, I think there's some stuff you both need to sort through."

"Yeah, I guess."

"Look B, I'm serious. I think he got his pride hurt, and now he's defaulting to his old tendencies. Do you think you can look past that? Is there something there that is worth all the crap you've been through?"

Bronwyn paused and thought for a long time, before she finally said, "I'd like to think that there could be."

"Well, there's your answer."

"Yeah, but…"

"But what? There's another girl? So what? There's a convoluted history you guys have? Well, that's one thing she doesn't have."

Bronwyn sighed, and changed the subject, "So, Joe, really?"

On her end, Lucy smiled and said, "What can I say? I love to be in love."

"And you didn't meet him while you were at Forrest Hills?"

"That's the weird thing – we never crossed paths. I mean, maybe he came to see Drew perform once or twice, but nothing official."

"If I come up, can I meet him?"

"*When* you come up, you definitely will." Lucy continued, "So, are we cool?"

"Yeah. But you'll let me know if Drew says anything to Joe? I need all the help I can get right now!"

"No problem. Take care, Bronwyn."

"You too."

To say the transition during the week following auditions was awkward was a huge understatement. J.D., in all his machismo, decided he wasn't going to pass up the opportunity to personally tell the Brass Captain that someone in his section was deferring to the Line. Bronwyn, frustrated by J.D.'s leadership (or lack of) and apparent goal to make this season the most difficult ever, decided not to do or say anything. She felt the worst for the seniors in her section – even if this year was terrible, she still had two seasons left.

Everyone in the band heard the argument between the Captains on Tuesday afternoon when the news broke. Geoff was in J.D.'s face, "I don't know where you get off, man!"

J.D. asked innocently, "What exactly is the problem?"

"Stealing a member of my section this late in the season? Seriously uncool, dude."

"He came to us."

"You didn't have to take him. You already have plenty of drummers."

"Well, he's got the chops. He's one of us now."

The repercussions of J.D. and Geoff's conversation had made an even more uncomfortable transition within the Line itself. There was some obvious resentment directed at Tony from the basses, who weren't entirely happy with his decision to become a snare drummer. Pete was going through much the same thing from the Brass players. While Tony only had to deal with negative feelings from four people, Pete had to walk the gauntlet through the band room on a daily basis. When her friend finally switched to Advanced Percussive Techniques on Thursday, it was obvious to Bronwyn that he was second-guessing his decision to swap sections. Besides herself, he hadn't received a particularly warm welcome from anyone on the Line. The bass drummers, already frustrated by losing one of their own, had short tempers when it came to the extra practices and sectionals required to get Pete up to speed.

By Thursday's practice, emotions in the band were at an all time low and Bronwyn wondered if it was too late to take things back. The brass players would have nothing to do with the members of the drum line. Whether or not they believed in J.D.'s decision to recruit Pete, their Captain's actions forced the percussionists together to defend themselves as a section. Unfortunately, it was putting further strain on a season that had already seen its fair share of frustration. Instead of one band, one sound, it was like a silent war. The band director, instructors, Drew, and the other drum majors were powerless to stop the bad feelings from circulating.

Although it had only been two days since the clash of the Captains, it seemed already every other section in the band was picking a side in the Line vs. the Brass battle. The neutrality from the drum majors just made matters worse – they refused to pick sides in the struggle between the sections, and wouldn't address the situation. Looking up at the drum major podium at the end of the ballad, Bronwyn was pretty sure Drew was going to be pro-Brass.

What would give you that idea?

Let's see, he used to play Mellophone, he hates me…

***Allegedly** hates you. Just because he ignored you **one** time does mean he is full of hatred for you. Remember what Lucy told you?*

Either way, he also hates J.D. and who wouldn't after what happened?

True.

So, it's somehow going to come down to the Line vs. the Band. What an optimistic outlook for the competitions ahead.

Maybe now is the time to talk to Drew. See if you can't get him to be impartial at least.

Once she had come to the decision that the peace of the band rested on her small shoulders, Bronwyn was determined to talk to Drew directly after practice that day. However, the entire afternoon session was an uphill battle that seemed to drag on for hours. There was constant verbal abuse between the leadership of the Brass and the senior percussionists. In addition to learning the new drill, Pete was also having to watch every step. Already irritated, Bronwyn's last water break was broken by a rough tug on her shirt. She turned around and looked at who had rudely approached her.

"What gives?"

Bronwyn squinted her eyes, trying to figure out what the hell the girl in front of her was referring to. She finally asked, "What are you talking about?"

Dana, in her matching maroon shorts and beige shirt, inspected her nails and said, "You know what I mean."

Bronwyn had had enough bad energy this week to last an entire season. She said tartly, "No, I don't."

"Like, you could've helped get me the spot."

"And how would've I done that?"

"You're a girl."

Bronwyn sighed loudly and spoke slowly, "I'm a drummer first."

"That's messed up."

"Well, Tony and Pete were the best players."

"Haven't I seen you and Pete together before?"

"He's my friend."

"Really? A friend?" Dana's tone implied that she didn't believe for one second that they were "just friends."

"It was a blind audition. You weren't good enough. Get over it and practice for next year." Bronwyn walked away, more than ready for the current week to be over.

Less than a half hour later, Bronwyn put Stewie away, then caught Ben and asked, "Can I meet you at the car? There's someone I need to talk to."

"Don't take too long."

Trying to put everything out of her head, Bronwyn walked calmly across the parking lot to a familiar car. She didn't want Drew to think she was stalking him, so she waited until he was halfway across the parking lot before she started walking towards him.

"Hey Drew!"

The drum major turned around, silently cursing the smile that broke across his face when he saw Bronwyn approaching him. He immediately tried to replace it with a nonchalant look, "What's up?"

"Well, so...I know things in the band are a little stressed right now."

"No thanks to, once again, your section."

Bronwyn shrugged, "Yeah, I guess."

"So?"

"I was wondering if well, maybe you could—"

"Oh Drew..." a female voice called from behind them.

The pair spun around and Bronwyn watched helplessly as Christina came walking across the parking lot.

"Oh..."

Drew crossed his arms, "Well, it's not like—"

At the same time Bronwyn said, "I'd better go."

Ben shouted across the parking lot, "Come on, B!"

Drew tapped his foot impatiently and said, "Shouldn't you be going, wouldn't want to keep your—"

"I'm leaving!" Bronwyn interjected.

As the sophomore walked away, she heard Christina tell Drew, "That's the girl who wouldn't let Dana on the Line."

Bronwyn was more than glad the following day marked the end of the week. Friday lunches were traditionally "cadence days" for the Line. The tradition had started long ago where the Battery would march into the Commons of the school and play as loud as they could for each lunch period on the day of a big football game to get everyone pumped up. For a few minutes, Bronwyn was able to forget the disastrous season so far, and concentrate on having fun – losing herself in the infectious beats. When they weren't worried about every note being clean, or precision marching, being a member of the Battery was actually an enjoyable experience. All eyes of the Commons were staring at the Line. Although she wasn't supposed to smile, Bronwyn couldn't keep the grin off her face.

By the last lunch, everyone on the Battery was relaxed and despite the week they had all shared, were actually having a good time together. Bronwyn looked out into the crowd and unexpectedly met Drew's blue eyed stare. Her heart momentarily stopped. There was so much more she had wanted to say to him yesterday. Without thinking through her actions, Bronwyn flashed a quick wink at him. At the very same moment, from the corner of her eye, she saw something whizz past her left side and *SPLAT!* right in the middle of Pete's bass drum head.

J.D. abruptly ended the cadence and the Line walked back silently to the band room. As soon as everyone had their drums off, they were busy looking at Pete's drum, which was now home to a large slice of cheese pizza. Their Captain yelled, "Stupid brass players! Who do they think they are?"

Bronwyn took a deep breath and, attempting to control the situation, asked calmly, "Did anyone actually see who threw the pizza?"

The band room was silent. Everyone looked around at each other. Bronwyn continued, "Then how do we know it was a brass player that threw it?"

Tony muttered, "Well, we know *you* wouldn't be a reliable source. You were too busy making eyes at Drew."

Bronwyn sputtered, "I was not!"

Tony said skeptically, "Sure."

J.D. glanced at the clock and put his hands up, "Enough, you two. I know for a fact Geoff has this lunch period, so I wouldn't be surprised if it was a good-for-nothing brass player. Keep your ears open, if you hear anything, let me know. Now, everyone needs to pack up their instruments. We've got an away game tonight."

Bronwyn walked into the snare section of the percussion room and pulled out her instrument case. She heard J.D. whisper to Lance, Scott, and Adam, "Hey guys…emergency meeting. Pre-game at Waffle House. We need to talk retaliation."

The three other snares nodded.

Adam nodded in the direction of Bronwyn and Tony, "What about those two?"

J.D. responded, "Upperclassmen only."

Bronwyn turned away, livid. After everything that had happened, after the many hours she had put into things, the time wasted trying to get their acceptance, there it was – obviously never going to happen.

Chapter Fourteen

If You're On Time (You're Five Minutes Late)

Bronwyn caught a ride with Ben to the game that evening. She was still in a funk from being excluded from the snare emergency meeting and in a horrible mood from the overall crummy week. Bronwyn brought Stewie outside and went immediately to the buses, surprisingly relieved to ride with the rest of Line. Last year, she had felt so much at home in the band, but now… everything was a big mess. Pete had also managed to switch buses, which was good considering Jared was already drilling his section and running through the show. Bronwyn looked around for someone to sit with and Ben gave her a sympathetic look. She sighed, relieved, and sat down next to her chauffeur.

The bus cranked up and Bronwyn looked around, realizing she was missing a few members of her section. She asked Mark, "Where's Lance?"

Mark shrugged, "He mentioned something about meeting J.D. before the game."

"Uh, J.D.'s not here either," said Steve.

Moments later, everyone stopped drumming as Mr. Izzo got on the bus. He cleared his throat and said, "Has anyone seen J.D., Lance, Scott or Adam?"

Everyone shook their head and turned their heads to Bronwyn. She volunteered, "Sorry, I have no idea where they are."

Her response was obviously not the answer Mr. Izzo was looking for. The band director looked at his watch, then addressed the percussionists, "I hate to do this, guys, but we have to leave without them. If you hear from them, please let me know."

Bronwyn's heart dropped to the bottom of her stomach. Without even realizing it, she turned and looked at Tony. Her fellow sophomore looked as if someone had punched him in the stomach. Unless the missing quartet showed up at the game, they had both realized that they would be the only snares marching the show. As the bus pulled away from the school, Mark's cell phone rang. He scrambled to find it and obviously recognized the caller. The bus was instantly quiet, intently listening to Mark's half of the conversation.

"Hello?"

"No shit dude – is everyone okay?"

"Yeah, we will."

"Who?"

"Yeah, she's here."

Mark pointed at Bronwyn and said, "It's J.D. He wants to talk to you."

Bronwyn nervously answered, "Hello?"

J.D.'s voice responded tersely, "B, we're not going to make it to the game."

"What happened?"

"Car accident—"

"Is everyone okay?!"

"Yeah, we're all fine, but there's no way we're going to be able to get to the game tonight. So, you're going to have to lead the Line."

Bronwyn squeaked, "Me?"

"Yes. Tony's too new and I won't let anyone but someone I trust to do it. If anyone gives you any crap, just tell them to call me."

"And you're sure Henry's not going to make it?"

"Yes."

There was no time to think. She scanned her brain for the answer J.D. wanted to hear, "I'll do my best."

"You'd better. Remember this isn't a night off. We have competitions coming up. I have to go."

Bronwyn heard a dial tone in her ear. She slowly closed the phone, realizing that everyone's eyes were on her. She stood up on the bus, took a deep breath and spoke clearly, "J.D., Lance, Adam, and Scott have been in a car accident. Everyone is okay, but they will not be able to make the game tonight. J.D. has asked that in his and Henry's absence that I lead the Line."

Everyone started immediately talking.

Bronwyn put her fingers to her mouth and whistled. Loudly. Everyone stopped their conversations. She continued, "It's going to take all of us tonight. We're not exactly the most popular section of the band right now, so we need to stick together. I expect you will give me the same respect and courtesy that you give both J.D. and Henry."

There was silence.

Jared was the first to comment, "You got it, B."

Ben said, "No worries."

Pete added, "We'll do it."

Not bothering to wait for the other confirmations, Bronwyn looked over at Tony and stated, "You. We're going to need to practice for the rest of the ride."

Tony nodded mutely.

The ride flew by and Bronwyn didn't even have time to think about being nervous or leading the Line. She was concentrating all her energy on getting Tony ready to march the show and trying to will some of her confidence to him. Unfortunately, Tony kept messing up a lick from the opener. Repeatedly. He finally threw his sticks down in frustration and yelled, "I can't do this! Can we please just water it down?"

Bronwyn gritted her teeth, collected his drum sticks, and said forcefully, "No, we are going to play the part as written. Let's show the Brass what a bunch of sophomores can do. You *can* do this. I've seen you do it a million times."

This was an out and out lie, but Bronwyn didn't think stretching the truth would hurt that much. As they pulled up to the opposing high school, Bronwyn nervously pulled on her uniform and willed her nervous feelings away. She could do this. J.D. had chosen her, and she wasn't going to let him down. As she got off the bus, Jared and Andy handed her their Lieutenant braids which they had fashioned into a large awkward plait. The bass Lieutenant said, "It's not much."

Bronwyn grinned and accepted the 'gift' graciously, "Thanks, guys. I know either one of you would probably be better at this."

Andy said, "I have another year and plenty of time to be Captain."

Jared replied, "Yeah, 5th bass leading warm ups? I think not."

She took a deep breath and approached Mr. Izzo, who was talking to Drew and Samantha, "Hey."

They all looked at her strangely. Bronwyn suddenly wished she were a little bit taller, but squared her shoulders and announced, "J.D. has named me de facto Captain for tonight. I just want to let everyone know the Line won't let you down."

Samantha asked skeptically, "You're marching two out of six snares? One of whom just joined the section *and* your Instructor isn't around?"

Bronwyn said plainly, "Yes."

Mr. Izzo thought a moment and said, "You know, we can just have the set player in the Pit keep time."

"No!" Bronwyn exclaimed.

The drum majors and band director looked strangely in her direction. Bronwyn continued in a more civilized tone, "I mean, it's under control. We're ready. I can handle this."

"You'll do fine," said Drew.

With Drew's encouragement, Bronwyn lit up. They watched her walk away. The senior drum major had a smile on his face as he watched her brave figure retreat.

At the equipment truck, Bronwyn pulled out Stewie and zipped her carrier under her uniform. She figured she should be more nervous, but all her emotions went away when she put on her drum. She called out to the Battery, "You know the drill, guys. Let's do it up!"

When the Line gathered, it became obvious to the rest of the band that something was amiss. A distinctly female voice called out loudly, "Eight on a hand...follow my lead!"

The crisp notes from the snare counted out the warm up and the Line began. Bronwyn held up her stick to signify the end of the warm up, "Great job guys, let's head to the stands."

Like any game, the home band was responsible for playing the National Anthem. The Line stood at perfect attention while they did. The first quarter went by faster than any fifteen minutes Bronwyn had ever remembered and suddenly it was time to go down to the field and warm up. Bronwyn kept a serious face, but on the inside she was jumping for joy. It felt so right to be leading the Line, but the big test was still ahead. After their warm-ups, the band lined up on the far side of the field. Bronwyn forgot that when the band marched out for the opening set, the snares lined up very close to Geoff and the rest of the trumpet section. And with the right half of the snare line gone, he was literally right next to her.

As everyone got in place and waited for the halftime buzzer to sound, she attempted to make conversation, "Hey Geoff..."

Although they were both supposed to be at attention, he looked down and asked, "Bronwyn, is it?"

She nodded. They shared a very random look and were interrupted when Drew coughed right in front of them. Bronwyn immediately shot her eyes forward. Drew nodded and asked, "The beat, Captain?"

Calmly, Bronwyn began tapping out quarter notes to keep everyone's left foot hitting the ground at the same time. Once the band was in place, Drew called everyone to attention and the show began. Bronwyn played as loud as she could, trying to compensate for the missing snares. Tony actually performed decently and between the two of them, they marched a pretty clean show. The pair shared a smile as they brought their sticks down at the end of the closer.

Bronwyn carefully settled Stewie and walked over to the concession stand for the third quarter. With her unapologetic and successful performance as

Captain, she was the new hero of the Forrest Hills Drum Line. It was a good feeling.

If only I had known that's all it would take to gain acceptance, I would have arranged for a car accident a long time ago!

Would J.D. have trusted you then?

Until now, Bronwyn hadn't really considered the impact of J.D.'s decision. There were many other upperclassmen or section leaders he could have chosen – but he picked her. That alone said more about how he really felt. For the first time in the season, Bronwyn felt really good about her place in the Line. She caught up to Mark and asked, "Have you heard anything from Lance or J.D.?"

"Nah, but I'm sure they're okay."

Watching Mark walk away, Bronwyn found herself alone, when someone approached her. She turned around and was surprised to see Geoff standing next to her. They both leaned on the fence surrounding the track.

"Good job tonight. Too bad you aren't in charge of the Line all the time."

Bronwyn's keen eyes swept over the band, enjoying their break time. She didn't want to, but her gaze was drawn to the new golden couple, holding court with the seniority of the band. Drew and Christina. Then she realized she still hadn't responded to Geoff's comment, and finally replied, "Thanks! I guess things got a little out of control this week."

"I just still can't believe Pete would…"

Bronwyn interrupted, "Would what? Want to be a drummer? It's not like he's dead – you have to cut the kid some slack."

"Yeah, but he was a strong player."

"I know. He's already a strong player for us."

Geoff sighed and finally said, "Y'know, I could let everything go. If only J.D. wasn't—"

"Such a dick?"

Geoff turned to look sideways at her, a mixture of surprise and approval on his face, and said, "You took the words right out of my mouth."

"Well, take it from someone who knows."

"Let me know if he ever crosses the line…"

Bronwyn couldn't help herself, "Then what? You'll cross the Line?"

Geoff hung his head and said, "That was terrible, but seriously just let me know."

Bronwyn said softly, "I will."

Balancing a Coke and some popcorn, Bronwyn returned to the stands and was almost back to the Line when she overheard Dana say, "Yeah well, to get Captain tonight, I heard she—"

What Bronwyn heard next was the most ludicrous and perverted thing ever –

which was a lot, considering she was a member of the drum line.

You're in uniform. You're the Captain of the Line. You cannot punch her in the face.

This is my reputation we're talking about. I don't want people thinking—

Do you trust your Line?

Yes.

Will they believe this kind of slander?

No.

There's your answer.

The look on Bronwyn's face must've told Ben and Mark everything. They weren't the only ones watching. A familiar pair of blue eyes were focused on Bronwyn as well.

Ben was immediately at Bronwyn's side, "This way, Captain."

Bronwyn forced a smile on her face, when all she really wanted to do was thrust her head into Dana's face.

"But she—"

"Shake it off, B," said Mark.

"I wanna—"

"Now's not the time, Bronwyn," said Ben.

Having missed their friend during the third quarter, Meredith and Megan had been looking for Bronwyn. Seeing the stormy look on her face, they immediately rushed to her side. Meredith looked at Ben shyly and said, "We got it from here, boys."

Megan said, "Thanks for your help."

Bronwyn allowed herself to be led to where the Pit was seated, far away from the other sections. Megan asked, "So, what happened exactly? I thought you'd be happy. Everyone's been talking about how well you did."

Bronwyn grappled for the right words. Finally, she sputtered, "It's not about that, apparently, Dana believes, well... She, she—" After finally whispering the implied and completely unfounded acts she had carried out to become Captain for a night, Meredith and Megan were appropriately shocked and outraged on Bronwyn's behalf.

"How could she even..." Megan was blown away.

"I don't know. It just makes me feel sick." Bronwyn wiped away the one or two frustrated tears that had leaked out, and admitted angrily, "Tonight, I did good and now she's taken it away from me."

Meredith patted Bronwyn gently on the shoulder, "Everyone knows it's not true."

Seeing Drew climb up on the drum major podium, the redhead looked up and said, "Well, girls, one quarter to go. I just thought my first time as Captain would be less dramatic."

Her friends made their way back to their respective spots in the stands, while Bronwyn contemplated her next move. She glanced over at the Guard and rolled her eyes. She was still glaring when Tony nudged her, "What's the deal, B?"

Bronwyn looked at Tony, took a deep breath, then said, "Nothing. Just some stupid girls. Good job tonight."

"Yeah, by the way, thanks for helping me."

"No worries. The sophomore snares have to stick together." Bronwyn continued, "Now, pick a cadence and let's make some noise!"

Chapter Fifteen

Hollaback...Boy?

For the final fifteen minutes of the game, Bronwyn forced herself to concentrate on the stand's songs and cadences instead of her rapidly declining reputation. Fortunately, her technique worked and the fourth quarter went by quickly. The Flyers football team won, which helped divert some of the attention away from her, but when she was supervising the loading of the percussion equipment a group of Guard girls passed by giggling and whispering and her bad feelings quickly returned. Bronwyn willed the tears back until she got on the bus.

Standing with Christina, Drew watched the scene. He nudged the Guard Captain, "Who are they talking about?"

Christina's perfectly arched eyebrows went up and she asked, "Why do you care?"

"Just wondering."

Dropping her voice low, she murmured, "It's about Bronwyn and well, apparently they're saying..."

As the girl he was dating revealed the sordid details, Drew's eyes widened, then darkened in anger. He could see now why Bronwyn had been so upset earlier in the evening. Not bothering to hide the rage in his voice, he asked, "Who the hell is behind that messed up rumor?"

Christina looked away and answered, "I'm not sure."

Drew crossed his arms, "Well, that's the most immature thing I've ever heard. I mean, everyone knows Bronwyn is a decent drummer. I'm sure J.D. had his reasons for choosing her."

"Isn't this the guy who revealed your evil plan to everyone? I thought you guys hated each other."

Drew said quickly, "We do. I just think it's crappy someone would mess with another person's reputation like that. Especially when it's not true."

"How can you be so sure?"

"Don't ask me how, I just know."

Closing his eyes, Drew was instantly brought back to the kiss he shared with Bronwyn. Surprising himself, Drew was secretly honored that he had given the pretty redhead her first kiss. He knew later in life Bronwyn would probably be a heartbreaker, and he was glad he got to be first on the list.

"Drew...?"

The drum major snapped back to reality, realizing Christina had asked him something, "What?"

As the bus pulled up to the school, the Line began cheering. Bronwyn looked out to the window to see what everyone was yelling about. Sitting in the parking lot were the missing snares: J.D., Lance, Scott, and Adam.

Bronwyn smiled to herself as they piled off the bus. Proving there was some hidden gallantry within him, J.D. took Bronwyn's snare case and, looking her up and down, commented, "You look like you've had a hell of a night. What happened?"

Too tired to get into the alienation of another section from the Line, Bronwyn shrugged and responded, "Nothing I couldn't handle."

J.D. nodded and they walked into the school together. The percussion room was full of band members trying to return their instruments to their upright and locked positions. J.D. nodded at Lance, who shut the door, "Alright, so let me fill you in on what happened. We were enjoying a little pre-game dinner at WaHo and decided we would all take one car over to the school. On the way, someone pulled out in front of us from nowhere and we kind of couldn't stop in time and ended up hitting them. The air bags deployed and we were all advised to go to the hospital. Seeing as though none of us want an injury to go unnoticed this close to competitions, we decided to go and get checked out and we're all fine."

The room was quiet, when Mark asked innocently, "So, who was driving?"

J.D. turned a very uncharacteristic shade of red.

Lance pointed to the drum line Captain and answered, "That would be him."

The semester continued forward, and it was apparent to everyone that the band was not overcoming their differences. For the first time in a long time, it looked as though the band might not come together and be a force for the upcoming competition. Drew, Geoff, and J.D. could just not agree on anything. Rivalry wasn't just concentrated within the leadership either. Bronwyn was finding new levels of patience she never knew she had... especially where persons named Dana and the Guard were concerned. She was finally gaining security on the Line, but the annoying looks and idle gossip were wearing on her patience.

To clear her head, the sophomore snare signed online, hoping to see Lucy's familiar screen name and was excited when the former bass drummer immediately wrote to her.

> **bassgirl17:** *Hey there!*
>
> **redheadedsnare:** *Hey yourself.*
>
> **bassgirl17:** *How's the season? I haven't heard from you in a while.*
>
> **redheadedsnare:** *Just dealing with rumors, nothing you haven't been through.*
>
> **bassgirl17:** *Eww... Want to elaborate?*
>
> **redheadedsnare:** *Not really – its just typical girl stuff. Also, the show is a complete disaster. All the sections hate each other, and Drew hasn't talked to me in weeks.*
>
> **bassgirl17:** *Dude...*
>
> **redheadedsnare:** *Don't get me started.*
>
> **bassgirl17:** *Why not? There's got to be a solution to at least one of these problems.*
>
> **redheadedsnare:** *...*
>
> **bassgirl17:** *No, seriously, I'm not getting offline until we've got something.*
>
> **redheadedsnare:** *I can't scheme any more! Not after what happened last time...*
>
> **bassgirl17:** *This time will be different. Now, which do you think is the most realistic to fix?*

Bronwyn thought a moment, trying to decide how the season could still be salvaged. Whatever J.D. and the senior snares had discussed at their botched trip to Waffle House had not materialized into anything specific. Furthermore, still smarting from the bet J.D. had made against her, the sophomore was unsure if she really wanted to do anything to help the remainder of the marching season. However, deep down, she knew some of the blame was hers. But, how to fix things? She typed frantically, hoping Lucy could help.

> **redheadedsnare:** *If I could just get Geoff and J.D. to get along, I think we might have a chance. If those two could get over themselves, maybe the band would start working together and then we won't have a colossal fail on our hands at the competitions.*
>
> **bassgirl17:** *OK, how can you arrange for that?*

> **redheadedsnare:** *I can't. They won't talk to each other. Because of Pete, basically they won't do anything together.*
>
> **bassgirl17:** *What if they didn't know they were doing something together?*
>
> **redheadedsnare:** *How do you mean?*
>
> **bassgirl17:** *Come up with some activity that has them agree or work together. Just make sure they don't know.*
>
> **redheadedsnare:** *Yeah, but seriously, what can one person actually do?*
>
> **bassgirl17:** *Correct me if I'm wrong, but isn't one person basically responsible for all of this?*
>
> **redheadedsnare:** *Maybe.*
>
> **bassgirl17:** *Well, maybe you can be the one to fix it.*
>
> **redheadedsnare:** *Why me?*
>
> **bassgirl17:** *Why not you? Look, you don't want to look back and regret **not** doing anything. I think more often, people regret why they did not do vs. what they did do.*
>
> **redheadedsnare:** *Call me pessimistic, but do you have an example?*
>
> **bassgirl17:** *Sure. Even though things with Drew didn't end the way you wanted them to, you would've never gone on the date with him if you hadn't tried. Do you really regret asking for his help?*
>
> **redheadedsnare:** *Fine, point made. I'll think about it.*

Lucy's comments forced Bronwyn to think about the season. On Sunday evening, the sophomore was getting ready for bed and listening to the radio, when she had a sudden burst of inspiration. She immediately called Pete and walked him through her idea. It didn't take much to convince him to help. As part of the cause of the rift between the sections, Pete was eager to help where he could.

The following morning, Bronwyn woke up feeling optimistic about the upcoming week. She was no closer to fixing things between herself and Drew, but damned if she hadn't come up with the perfect solution to the division between the Brass and the Line. Bronwyn caught up with the senior, "Hey J.D.?"

"What's up, She-Captain?" He was using his new nickname for her, which Bronwyn supposed was a compliment.

"I've got something for Friday."

"Really?"

"Yup, something different. I worked it out over the weekend." She dug into her backpack and pulled out the music she had hastily written for each section.

J.D. looked intrigued as he reviewed the arrangement, "What do you call it?"

Bronwyn shrugged and replied hesitantly, "Hollaback?"

"I like it."

"Can we play it on Friday?"

"What's the rush?"

"No reason, I just thought we could do something new. I think everyone can learn it at sectionals."

"I'll think about it."

The next afternoon was the Tuesday before the first competition of the season and the Brass and Line were no closer to solving their differences. Bronwyn knew she had to make her move soon. She and Pete had hastily arranged the music as best they could – Pete had found the Brass parts and Bronwyn had arranged the corresponding percussion section. Now came the tough part. At the last minute, Bronwyn decided she would be the one to talk to Geoff. He was a pivotal part of their plan and without his involvement, they wouldn't have a chance.

Pete asked, "So, what are you going to say?"

"Think like a guy, Pete. Geoff won't go along with this unless he thinks J.D. thinks he won't."

"Huh?"

Bronwyn smiled and said, "I go up to Geoff and tell him J.D. has been thinking of doing this new thing for Friday's lunch, but doesn't think the Brass are up to it. Now do you understand?"

Pete nodded slowly and said, "Yes?"

"Plus, I don't remember you and Geoff being the best of friends right now."

"True."

"So, the best thing you can do for me right now is convince J.D. to play Hollaback on Friday." Bronwyn nudged Pete in the direction of J.D. as she went in search of Geoff on the way down to the practice field. Finding the handsome brass Captain was easy enough. He was in the middle of drilling some of the trombones through a complicated section of the show. Approaching him was something different entirely. Without thinking through her options, she popped her drumstick on her snare head and watched as it went flying right to Geoff's feet. He raised an eyebrow, but picked it up and walked over to her, calling back behind him, "Take five, guys."

He asked, "This yours?"

Bronwyn smiled flirtatiously, "Oops, sorry about that."

Geoff turned to leave and awkwardly Bronwyn asked, "Umm…I have a question for you."

"Yeah?"

It was now or never. "Well, I heard J.D. talking about this thing he wants to do for the Friday lunch period."

Geoff's attention was piqued, "Yeah? What would that have to do with me?"

"I heard he put together this new cadence, but it really needs a brass part."

The senior considered her comment for a beat and then said, "Forget it. You know where you can tell your Captain to put it."

"Yeah, that's what he said you'd say," Bronwyn turned and started walking away, "Too bad though."

3…2…1…

"What is it?"

Bronwyn turned back to Geoff and asked, "You've heard of the song *Hollaback Girl*, right?"

Geoff nodded, "Yeah, it's got a decent horn line."

"That's the one! Anyway," she dug the music out of her pocket, "Pete arranged the brass part, so at least you know he knows what he's doing."

Geoff took the music and said, "We'll see."

"Just one more thing. Let's pretend we didn't have this conversation. If you decide to do it, just show J.D. and the rest of the Line in the Commons during Friday's lunch."

"Sounds like my kind of plan."

From across the field, Drew wondered exactly what that conversation had been about. The brass Captain and redheaded snare had been spending quite enough time together recently.

Why should you care? You're dating Christina, remember?

I don't care.

Then why are you still staring?

I'm not.

Then why have you noticed?

I haven't.

After conferring with Pete, Bronwyn kept her fingers crossed that things would come together on Friday. It was risking a lot, but something *had* to persuade these guys to get along again. Thursday's practice showed promise, but by no means proved that the Forrest Hills Flyers marching band was going to win any particular captions at competition. In need of something remotely optimistic, Bronwyn was happily surprised when Ben mentioned to her during practice, "We're going to be taking Meredith home tonight…"

Bronwyn, not one to stand in the way of anyone's romance, said quickly, "I just remembered, I have to stay late and help Tony."

Ben looked like he didn't quite believe her, "Sure…"

Bronwyn nodded enthusiastically, "It's true! You think I *want* to help Tony?"

Ben smiled, "Okay, I believe you."

If Bronwyn's plan was destined not to be a success on Friday, she was determined to go down looking good. She borrowed extensively from Megan and Meredith's closets and decided on a flirty black skirt, white button up long sleeve shirt, and skinny tie. Fifth period came entirely too soon, and Bronwyn held her breath as the Line prepared to march into the Commons.

J.D. looked at everyone and said, "So, we're going to give Bronwyn's Hollaback a try. Let's march in with Spyder, then I'll cue Hollaback."

Bronwyn released a large sigh of relief and met Pete's happy look. Part One of the plan completed! As they marched into the Commons, Bronwyn could see some Brass members gathered where the Line usually parked and drummed. She looked over and grinned when she saw Geoff and some of the upperclassmen of the brass had their instruments in hand.

The second J.D. prepped to count off for the new song, Geoff and the rest of the brass players stood up and began playing their parts of the music. The Line was too shocked to do anything but keep playing, and were even able to enhance their part when the cymbals quickly joined the snares. Geoff had gone further with the arrangement and was playing the vocal line as a solo. The students in the Commons area went crazy! Then, out of nowhere, the Varsity cheerleaders in the lunch period got up and started doing a routine along to the music. Bronwyn had no idea how the events had come together, but was excited beyond belief.

Too soon, the song was over and the Line was marching back to the band room, with Geoff and the brass players following.

Bronwyn held her breath as they all collected together.

J.D. looked over at Geoff, tucked his sticks under his arm, and extended his hand, "Truce?"

Geoff extended his own hand and the guys shook, "Truce."

The second they stopped shaking, everyone in the band room went ballistic. Bronwyn sat back and watched the two sections congratulate each other. For a part time schemer, she wasn't too bad. Pete, surrounded by his former section, flashed her a quick smile. When Bronwyn made her way into the percussion room, Geoff and J.D. approached her.

J.D. asked, "Bronwyn?"

She answered tentatively, "Yes?"

Geoff questioned, "Was this your idea?"

She contemplated telling them it was Pete, but decided it was her turn to tell the truth, "Yup. All the way."

J.D. looked content, then asked, "But how did you get the cheerleaders to go for it?"

Without a clue how to answer that question, Bronwyn just shrugged and answered, "A girl's got to have her secrets."

J.D. smiled, "Well, we've decided we are going to do this next lunch and for the last lunch we want you to sing the actual vocals."

Bronwyn shook her head violently, "No way! I'm a drummer, not a singer."

J.D. laughed and said, "I thought you might say that, how about you and Geoff solo in front of all of us?"

Bronwyn thought a moment, she'd earned a moment in the spotlight. She finally smiled and said, "Okay…"

By the last lunch, there was a buzz in the lunchroom as the Line marched in. Apparently, word had gotten around that things were extra loud today. Bronwyn was slightly nervous at being at the front, but when she realized a) no one could hear her and b) were probably concentrating on the cheerleaders anyway, she started singing the lyrics. After a while she got caught up in the song and she and Geoff started improvising a crazy dance. Well, as much as two people could dance wearing drums and playing brass instruments could. For once, Bronwyn sighed with relief, her plans were more successful than even she could have imagined.

Chapter Sixteen

With A Little Help From My Friends

Bronwyn walked out of her house to catch her ride to the school that night with Ben. Unsurprisingly, the tenor player was still curious about what happened earlier in the day, "That was so bad ass. How did you pull it off?"

By third lunch, Bronwyn had chalked it up to serendipity. She answered, "Just lucky, I guess."

"I heard Henry's due back tonight."

"I'm sure he'll have a lot to say," she replied diplomatically. Bronwyn secretly questioned just how "cool" their instructor was going to be with J.D.'s decisions over the past couple of weeks. To return and find one member of the snare line had been replaced by a bass player, and that a brass musician was currently on the bass line would be strange information.

What's done is done…at this point it's not like Henry can switch everything back.

Rather than gossip about her section mate, Bronwyn had something much more important to ask, "So, how are things going with Meredith?"

Ben looked pointedly at her.

"What? You get to ask me personal stuff! Why can't I ask you?"

"Hasn't she told you? I thought you two were supposed to be good friends."

"Well…I was kind of busy planning the whole Hollaback thing, so I didn't get to talk to her as much as I usually do."

"I guess it's going well."

"You guess?"

"I mean, you can't tell a lot from one car ride, B."

"Okay. Are you going to see her again?"

"For your information, Miss Nosy, we're going out on Sunday. Happy?"

Bronwyn smiled, "Yes. Now see, that wasn't so hard, was it?"

As a response, Ben grumbled something under his breath.

Like usual, Ben and Bronwyn arrived at the school much earlier than necessary and had plenty of time to goof around before warm ups. Bronwyn was treating herself to a pre-game Gatorade when she noticed Tony trying to get someone's attention. She watched Dana giggle and follow Tony down a deserted hall.

And here I thought he was actually capable of change...

Meredith walked up to her friend and followed Bronwyn's line of sight, "Do you think he knows she's probably only after him because in her warped mind she thinks she can improve her chances to get on the Line?"

Megan put her arm around Bronwyn and replied, "Well, that's too bad, because she already pissed off its future Captain."

Bronwyn smiled at both girls, before linking arms with them and walking off to the band room, "What's this I hear about you and Ben going out on Sunday?"

Upon arriving in the percussion room, J.D. announced a mandatory meeting out in front of the school for all drum line members. The Line was silent as they gathered. Bronwyn hadn't seen Henry in a while and wondered what he was going to say. J.D. was still alive, so that was a good start.

Henry wasn't usually much of a talker, but tonight it seemed he had a lot to say. He cleared his throat and began, "Hey guys. So, a few things to go over with you. When we started this season, I mentioned how much of the leadership graduated with last year's class and how you would all have to step up your game. Now, I didn't plan on being gone as long as I had to be. As this is my sixth season as instructor of this Line, I've seen a lot of talent come and go. I've also learned that as difficult a part I can write, or as much as we can practice, when it comes down to it, *you* are the ones playing the notes and the decisions you make, well, all of it adds up to be *your* Line. While I respect J.D. as Captain, would I have pulled the first bass to move up to snare? Probably not. But these are decisions we cannot reverse and must go forward with. So, as we go into competition tomorrow, just remember that in life we don't always make the right decisions, but those of us who are smart enough, learn from our mistakes."

Bronwyn smiled to herself and wished she could be as diplomatic as Henry when it came to thoughts of J.D. or Dana. It also made her think about Drew – and not for the first time in the semester she wished she could go back in time and make the right choice – not to get involved in the first place. Bronwyn looked around and noticed the usually rambunctious Line was quiet, contemplating what Henry had just said.

Henry smiled and continued, "Now that that's out of the way, I'd like you all to know that while I was gone, I finished writing the Indoor show."

Everyone looked up eagerly.

"Even though this has been in my head for a while, I've been holding off, but I think maybe you guys are the Line to do it. We're doing selections from Holst's Planets Suite. Be ready, because it's going to take a lot of effort and practice to get it right."

The home game that evening marked a massive improvement in the band's relations and its overall performance quality. Everyone was still buzzing about the Brass/Line 'duet' in the Commons that lunchtime and the sections were encouraged by the crowd to play an encore. Bronwyn reprised her role with Geoff and the cheerleaders came over to the band section to join in.

To say the half-time show was the best run ever was an understatement. Even the crowd responded to the newly improved performance.

From the stands, Mr. Izzo stared in bewilderment at his band. At Thursday's rehearsal they hadn't performed nearly this well. He shook his head. That was the crazy and sometimes magical thing about working with high school students – they could surprise you when you least expected it.

As Drew slowly brought his hands down, he knew the show had been a success. From behind him, he heard the roar of the collected marching bands gathered for the Buccaneers Marching Classic.

J.D. tapped the notes on his snare to quickly get the band off the field.

As per usual, the stands were full and the Forrest Hills marching band had to wait on the sidelines for the results. After the two remaining bands performed, the Captains, Lieutenants and drum majors walked calmly out to the center of the field to await the results.

Bronwyn thought about the night's performance, recognizing that as far as they had come, there were still a number of amazing bands in the competition. She didn't realize until now how much they took winning, or placing in the top three, for granted. In these high stakes competitions, you couldn't blame rebuilding or injury, you just had to go out and march the best damn show you could. She knew all of these bands worked just as hard as Forrest Hills did – they had been sweating since August, they had put in long hours practicing out on the field. Bronwyn looked out over the field and saw that Geoff and J.D. were standing together – as if they had been best friends forever. Things were as they were supposed to be, but was it too late? Had the band come together in time? As much as she didn't want to, she also desperately tried not to notice Drew and Christina stood next to each other. In uniform, they looked even more perfect together, if that was possible.

Finally, it was time for their Class awards. The band was called to attention and, as luck would have it, Bronwyn had lined up near the proximity of the Guard.

Of all the sections to be lined up next to.

Just breathe…

She's standing right in front of me!

Although she projected to everyone else that she was over the incident, Bronwyn was still smarting from the rumors Dana started. She didn't think she was going to be letting go of that grudge any time soon. It was then she looked over and realized she was also standing next to Tony. Since the game last Friday there had been an uneasy truce between them. She wasn't about to forgive five years of verbal abuse in one night, but she was glad to see that there was a glimmer of hope that people could change. She looked over and tried to control a giggle when she saw Tony and Dana were making weird faces at each other.

Fortunately, Tony and Dana's bizarre mating habits were interrupted and it was time for the captions to be announced. As the competition organizers went through each category, each section was shocked and disappointed as the band failed to win even one caption. There were a few second and third place trophies collected, but nothing like their usual placements. Bronwyn saw seriously disappointed looks on the faces around her. When the High Percussion awards were called and the Line placed a mere third, it was like being punched in the stomach. The announcement forced Bronwyn to recognize the obvious, while she knew her part of the show was clean, she had been ignoring the rest of the Line and what she could do to help them. The negative mood this season had come from J.D., but why had she submitted to it? Leaders didn't have to have something special on their uniform – or be officially designated – they could just be the part.

The walk back to the equipment truck was an exceptionally quiet one. Bronwyn was especially sorry for the seniors. They only had one more chance to win. She thought about the drum line's portion of the show and some of the other breaks she had seen. The third place trophy was actually a nice gesture from the judges. From what she had heard, South Washington and Swiss County both looked better and played a cleaner show. Back on the bus, it was obvious everyone was feeling terrible about the evening's events.

Henry spoke briefly to the group, "Next week, guys. No worries."

Lance added, "I'm sure we can learn a lot from the judges tapes."

J.D. seemed especially pissed. Rather than be a good role model and boost everyone's morale, he was sitting and sulking in the last seat of the bus. Bronwyn secretly wondered what was going through her Captain's mind.

Maybe he's actually regretting his decision to bump Tony up…

Do you think he would actually admit it?

*This **is** J.D. we're talking about.*

I won't make the same mistake.

When?

When I'm Captain.

Although the atmosphere was sad, Bronwyn smiled to herself. By her senior year, she vowed to learn from those who came before her. She would have the strongest Line Forrest Hills had ever seen.

Although Mr. Izzo tried to reinforce what a great job the band had done, how far they had come, and how proud everyone should be – the mood in the band room was a quiet one. Returning Stewie to the percussion closet, Bronwyn knew there wasn't going to be a trip to Waffle House tonight. She and the girls had decided to have an impromptu sleepover. With duffel bags packed for any occasion, Meredith and Bronwyn didn't have to go home first. They waited in front of the school for Megan's mom to pick them up. Ben decided to be a gentleman and wait with them, which Bronwyn thought was a very nice gesture. She didn't realize she had been riding with a romantic all season.

At least there is some hope out there...

Around 3AM and halfway through their favorite card game, Bronwyn made an impromptu announcement, "Girls, I have to tell you something."

Megan whispered loudly, "You still like Drew."

Bronwyn sighed, then threw a pillow at her friend's head, "Aaaahhhh!! Is it that obvious?"

Meredith nodded, "Sorry, but yeah. You get all angsty every time he's around or his name is mentioned."

Bronwyn looked worried, "Do you think he knows?"

Megan replied, "Actually, I think it's only obvious to girls. Guys are completely oblivious to that kind of stuff."

After she played the next card in the series, Meredith asked, "What about Mr. Brass Captain? You guys look pretty cute together, and he's not dating anyone right now."

"He's nice enough, but it just kills me to see Christina and Drew. I think all of this is being made worse by the fact that skankity Dana and Tony were all lovey dovey in front of me tonight. It seems like everywhere I turn everyone is disgustingly happy. No offense, Mere."

"None taken."

Megan asked, "So you don't want to even try dating Geoff?"

"Do you really think he likes me that much?"

"I wish you could've seen yourself in the stands last night."

"Was I that bad?"

Meredith laughed, "Well, I can see where he might be getting the idea that you like him."

Megan joined her friends laughing and said, "I think the whole band could see that."

Bronwyn put down the winning card and said, "Did I ever tell either of you that I had no idea my 10th grade year was going to turn out like this?"

Meredith answered, "Well, I seem to remember you saying you wanted things to be different this year."

"Remind me to keep my big mouth shut next time."

Chapter Seventeen

Accelerando

After sleeping in the following day, Bronwyn went home feeling significantly relieved she had finally shared the "secret" that she wasn't quite over Drew like she had been trying to convince herself she was. That being said, now that the information was out there, she still had no idea what to do with it. The end of the season was in sight, and as a sophomore, Bronwyn wouldn't have many opportunities left to interact with Drew after November.

Bronwyn walked into the percussion period on Monday, not exactly sure what the tapes from the competition were going to say. As a freshman, and a member of the Pit last year, she hadn't been so keenly aware of what the tapes highlighted. However, last year, the show had been amazing and they had received firsts left, right and center. Former quint Lieutenant Tom had been so proud of the first competition tape that he had it framed and it was placed above the door of the percussion room. It had even become a tradition that before a competition, the drummers would touch it for good luck. The sophomore snare had a feeling the tapes today were not going to be so kind.

Before starting the first tape, J.D. addressed the other members of the Line, "If any one of you is mentioned specifically by a judge in this thing… you get laps before practice tomorrow. Don't think I'm not serious."

Bronwyn doubted she had anything to really worry about. She knew she had played a very clean show.

With the sounds of the crowded stands and announcer in the background, the judge's voice carried over, "…Always look forward to hearing the Forrest Hills drum line. Let's see what you have for me tonight."

Bronwyn heard Drew count the band off and the show started. She held her breath until the drum solo. The snare solo was very close to being clean however, she could hear someone lagging just a little bit.

"…quints great job, snares….solo…almost clean, looks like one of you on the end has a little more work to do."

The judge frantically talked his way through the entire show. As the closer came to a finish, the judge had one more remark, "Oh, what's this? First bass is off step."

While the judge wrapped up his comments about the overall performance, J.D. looked at a notepad he had been frantically scribbling on. There were only two snares "on the end," Bronwyn and Tony. There was only one first bass, Pete. With how close the drum line captions were, it could've been those small things that had lost first place for the Line. J.D. put the notebook down and said, "Let's start with the snares."

Tony was the first to speak, and put his hands up, "No way dude, you don't actually think it was me, do you?"

Bronwyn was flabbergasted. She was sure that Tony had messed up the solo. She could understand the pressure he was under in such a large band, with more than 5,000 people watching, and only six people playing…it was easy to drop notes or lose concentration.

Tony continued, "Look, Bronwyn can't even speak up. Obviously it was her."

Through clenched teeth she said slowly, "I did…not…f…up…the… solo."

J.D. looked at both of them.

Adam had sat by listening for long enough. He said, "Tony, believe me, I can vouch for Bronwyn. We were clean on the West Side."

Lance added, "There's no shame, dude. I mean you just joined the section like, a week ago."

Tony crossed his arms, "You all heard my audition. I *nailed* the solo."

Bronwyn threw her hands up in frustration, "I can't believe we're even *having* this conversation. I played the solo perfectly."

There's only way you're going to be able to prove this…

Bronwyn stood up, "Right now, Tony. You and me. Let's drum."

Tony looked wary for a moment before agreeing, "Fine."

Neither looked at J.D. for approval. Bronwyn angrily grabbed Stewie and her carrier, while Tony did the same. By the time they exited the percussion room, J.D. had cleared a space in the middle of the band room. He told the two sophomores, "If you're going to do this. You're going to do it with drill."

Bronwyn looked at the kitten heel flip flops she had put on that morning. Kicking them off, she said, "Fine by me!"

J.D. looked at both drummers, "On my count. The entire drum solo. Mark time, hut."

He clicked off the notes. The pair marched the drill effortlessly and as they reached the end of the break, Bronwyn knew she had played a more precise show – complete with visuals and the audio phrase they had added at the end.

When they finished, Tony and Bronwyn looked at J.D.

J.D. said stoically, "Tony, laps and push-ups tomorrow afternoon. Pete, you too."

Bronwyn resisted the urge to once again stick her tongue in Tony's face. Then she sighed, realizing it wasn't about playing better. The snare line was only as good as its weakest instrumentalist. Animosity in the section and across the band had earned the Flyers an overall fifth place finish – how hypocritical could she be? It was time to put her pride aside and deal with the situation.

Bronwyn was still questioning how to make things right as she walked down to the practice field the following afternoon. She saw Tony preparing for his run and felt guilty. Without thinking much through her actions, Bronwyn ran as fast as she could and joined him.

Tony looked at her strangely and said, "What are you doing?"

"What? I just felt like running."

"You're not helping."

As mad as Tony might have been, they ran in companionable silence the rest of the laps. Bronwyn's mind wandered as she ran. Henry, true to his word, had passed out the Indoor show music and she was surprised at the skill level he had written. She hoped that they would be able to perform to his expectations. Looking across the field, she made eye contact with Geoff and quickly looked away. After the sleepover with her friends, she realized the best thing to do would be to finish the season as a strong player of the snare line and nothing more. A relationship seemed like the perfect way to complicate the acceptance she had worked so hard towards.

Given that Homecoming is a mere three weeks away, most girls would be chatting a potential date up rather than running next to some jerk when they didn't have to.

I'm not most girls…

After an intensive week of rehearsals, Drew brought his hands down and the final "HUT!" was shouted back to him, echoing across the crowded stadium. He felt much better than he had a week ago. As his last competitive performance, he was proud of himself and the entire band – let the judges makes their own decisions, he knew it was the very best run of the show possible. If that wasn't good enough, the band could still take pride in what they had achieved.

Once settled on the track, the Forrest Hills marching band could only wait patiently until the scores were tallied. The perfect version of a show was such an intangible thing to measure. To have every section come together, to have the chemistry just right, to build the energy, to engage the crowd, it wasn't something that could be easily forced. Bronwyn was finally able to see what Mr. Izzo must have seen so many months ago. The potential of the show had always been there, but until tonight it had never come together. Would it be enough? She knew they were up against some particularly difficult competition. It seemed every band had brought their best game to the field that evening.

Unsurprisingly, the Forrest Hills band received all Superior ratings. Bronwyn held her breath as the captions were called. She was glad to hear some of the sections receive second and third place marks. When the announcer began calling the drum major caption, Bronwyn crossed her fingers. Even if she didn't have a chance at a relationship with him, she still wanted Drew to be successful.

"In third place, Benedictine High School."

"In second place, South Washington High School."

Bronwyn held her breath. With all the great performances during the day, the award could go to a few of the schools present.

"In first place, Forrest Hills High School!"

After hearing the drum major caption award going to Drew, Samantha and Alex, Bronwyn beamed with pride as she looked at the field. Then immediately wished she hadn't. She watched jealously as Christina give Drew a kiss on the cheek as he walked forward to receive his trophy. Luckily, Bronwyn's envy was quickly replaced by anticipation. The Line's category was next. She barely had time to hold her breath when the announcer said, "For High Percussion honors…in third place, Forrest Hills High School."

Bronwyn shared a look with the rest of the drummers. They watched J.D. strut out across the field and accept the trophy. If he was dissatisfied with the placement, he didn't let it show. Although Bronwyn was disappointed for the seniors, she felt third place was what they had earned…what they deserved after such a disruptive season. Maybe their book was more difficult than others, but their execution hadn't been perfect. In the end, she knew the judges had made the correct decision.

Overall, the band placed third and were happy to do so. After everything that had happened during the season, a third place finish was one everyone could be proud of. Bronwyn also realized that if the band won every year, what would push them to be better next season? Sometimes the challenge was trying to do the best with what you had. Given the talent that had graduated previously, she was happy with the results.

In the wee hours of the morning, when the band finally pulled into the familiar Forrest Hills parking lot, Bronwyn walked back towards the school with Stewie in one hand and her carrier and uniform bag in the other, and suddenly found herself walking next to Drew.

"Congratulations," she said softly, genuinely proud of his effort and leadership of the band.

"You too."

"Thanks."

"Bronwyn, I should tell you—"

He was cut off as Christina came around the corner and exclaimed, "There you are!"

The Guard Captain linked her arm through Drew's and she steered him in the opposite direction, leaving Bronwyn completely alone.

After safely putting Stewie away, Bronwyn met up with her friends and pretended to get caught up in their enthusiasm. She didn't feel like going to Waffle House to celebrate with the Line, so she caught a ride to Krispy Kreme with Ben and Meredith. Bronwyn watched jealously as she walked out with the pair, when Ben took Meredith's hand. Meredith said quietly, "B, I should tell you something."

"What's up?"

"I heard Drew asked Christina to Homecoming."

Was that was he was going to tell me?

"Oh."

"I just thought you should hear it from me."

Bronwyn sighed and said, "Thanks."

From across the parking lot, Drew watched the trio confused and a sinking feeling in the pit of his stomach. Judging from the body language, there was no way Ben was involved with Bronwyn. The tenor player was super attentive to the other girl with them, and friendly, at best, to the sophomore snare.

Geoff joined him and congratulated Drew, "Great job tonight."

"You too. I can't believe, well, it doesn't seem like it was our last."

"I know. Where are you headed tonight to celebrate?"

Drew shrugged and said, "I'm not sure, probably wherever Christina and the Guard goes."

The trumpet soloist shifted his instrument and asked, "Umm, Drew?"

"Yeah?"

"This is probably going to sound weird."

The pit in Drew's stomach grew even larger. Although he hadn't specifically seen any interaction between Bronwyn and the kid who drove her home, he wasn't blind. Ever since their little 'jam' in the Commons, Geoff and Bronwyn were practically all anyone could talk about. Although the potential pair was oblivious to all the band matchmakers, Drew assumed it was that everyone went a little crazy this close to Homecoming.

He finally answered, "Go ahead."

"So, what was up with you and Bronwyn earlier this season?"

Drew chuckled and said, "You wouldn't believe me if I told you."

"What does that mean?"

The drum major shook his head and answered honestly, "You know what? She's too good for me. I don't think I deserve a girl like Bronwyn Flueger."

"So…?"

Drew knew his friend was a good guy, as much as it pained him to think about Bronwyn with someone else, at least Geoff was worthy. Drew replied sadly, "Go for it, man."

Chapter Eighteen

I'll Never Fall in Love, Again

After his conversation with Geoff, Drew was very thankful he had encouraged Christina to take her own car that morning. With his rationale and judgment thrown completely out of whack, the drum major decided it would be best to appeal to his brother. He pressed the speed dial button, and as soon as he heard the call connect, said, "Dude?"

"What's up?"

"I think I screwed up."

On the other end of the phone, Joe sighed, "What did you do?"

"I think I asked the wrong girl to Homecoming."

"How is that even possible?"

"I don't know."

"Well, obviously you do, because you're telling me you have."

"So, I can't, um, un-ask someone?"

"Drew, you cannot reneg a Homecoming date. That's like, an unspoken rule."

Drew sighed, "It is?"

"Of course it is!"

"So what am I going to do?"

"You'd better go with the girl you already asked."

"Damn it. I thought that's what you were going to say."

"Sorry dude. Anything else?"

"No."

Drew hung up the phone, feeling miserable.

And here I thought I actually knew a thing or two about girls…

It would serve you right if Bronwyn goes with Geoff.

To: karatechop@state.edu
From: FHHSsnaregrl@FHHS.edu

Lucy,

Hey, so my parents aren't so much buying the whole "visiting" you at college. What I did manage to come up with is that I want to attend an advanced percussion clinic (which is for real and on Saturday afternoon in the music school with a respectable clinician) and that I'll just stay at your place for a night. Sound cool?

B

To: FHHSsnaregrl@FHHS.edu
From: karatechop@state.edu

B,

No worries. So, if you can get your parents to drive you up on Saturday, I'll bring you back on Sunday. Hopefully they'll agree to that plan.

And say, isn't it that time of year for certain people to be enjoying dances?

Luce

To: karatechop@state.edu
From: FHHSsnaregrl@FHHS.edu

Lucy,

I checked with my parents and they're cool with the whole clinic/driving thing. So, I'll see you in two weeks? I'm super looking forward to it!

*About that whole dance thing? Well, it's the same weekend as the clinic. The whole reason I'm coming up to see you is because I could **CARE LESS**.*

B

Clicking "send," Bronwyn hoped she would make it through the next two weeks. Maybe she hadn't been so clued up on things last year, but this year she realized people were literally *obsessed* with the dance.

Maybe if I was going with someone I really liked, I would understand the feeling…

By the last practice before the Homecoming game, it seemed everyone in the band was pairing off. Bronwyn had been genuinely excited to learn Ben had asked Meredith, and in a kind of last minute effort, Tyler had decided to escort Megan "as friends." Proving that *everyone* was going but her, she heard Tony was taking Dana.

With the competitive season over, and only the Homecoming arrangement to play, the band was taking it easy for the day. Megan absentmindedly twirled her flute, and asked, "Maybe you could go with Pete?"

Bronwyn scoffed, "Bad idea."

Meredith was lying flat on the grass, "Why?"

"Uh…" Bronwyn couldn't exactly explain to her friends the real reasons. She couldn't very well tell them a) she was completely against dating *anyone* in her section and b) if she was going to date someone in her section, it certainly wasn't going to be a transfer bass drummer.

Did I really just think that?

I'm turning into a section snob! J.D. has finally gotten through to me!

To her friends, she merely commented, "It would just complicate things too much. Plus, remember? I have the clinic."

With that, she leaned back on the grass of the practice field and stared up at the blue afternoon sky. She closed her eyes, enjoying herself, when she felt a shadow over her. Shielding her eyes, she opened them and saw someone, a tall male someone, looming above her.

Geoff asked, "Mind if I borrow her for a few minutes, ladies?"

Megan flushed, but answered flirtatiously, "Go for it. Just return her in good condition."

Geoff extended his hand and pulled Bronwyn up. Bronwyn was momentarily lost in watching his bicep contract and fell into him as she stood up. Geoff raised an eyebrow and commented to her friends, "See you soon."

"So…?" Bronwyn literally had no idea what to say to Geoff. She had enjoyed developing a friendship with him, but was still harboring major feelings for Drew.

"Bronwyn, I was wondering something."

"Yes?"

"Have you been avoiding me?"

Bronwyn didn't want to answer the question honestly, because she had totally been avoiding him. In her best effort of dealing with the crush vibes she felt coming from Geoff, she figured the best way to deal with it would be to just ignore them…and him.

"Umm, no."

"Huh."

"Why? Do you think I have?"

"Not exactly."

Geoff looked over at the little redhead walking next to him, "I was wondering…"

Bronwyn interrupted, "No."

"You don't even know what I was going to ask."

"You were going to ask me to Homecoming or on a date or something?" Bronwyn refused to look over at the trumpet player.

"Maybe."

Bronwyn felt thoroughly awkward, and wished she hadn't been so abrupt. Maybe being in the mostly male section was rubbing off on her.

You should give him a reason.

Won't that make it worse?

Could it get any worse?

Now that you mention it…not really.

Bronwyn tried to soften the blow, "It's just – I like someone else. I mean, we could go as friends, but…"

"Oh."

Bronwyn gave a deep sigh.

"What's up?"

Bronwyn suddenly found it amusing that although she was the one who had rejected Geoff, he was all compassionate about her dramatic sigh. Why couldn't she like him? Her life would be so much easier if she could just like him. She finally answered, "Things aren't going to be weird between us, are they?"

Geoff shook his head, "No."

"Promise?"

He bowed low and said, "As a pledge of how I promise it won't be weird, how about I give you a ride home from practice today?"

Bronwyn grinned, "Sounds great."

Drew tried not to notice Bronwyn climbing into Geoff's car that afternoon.

You had your chance.

And you blew it…

Drew could kick himself, remembering the sad look on Bronwyn's face that night she had approached him in the parking lot.

Why didn't I just hear her out?

With fall in full force, the Homecoming game was chilly. Bronwyn carefully dressed in layers. Looking back, it had been an exhausting two weeks and she was looking forward to relaxing with Lucy over the weekend. After learning the Homecoming song ("Come What May" from *Moulin Rouge!*)

and its corresponding drill, J.D. and Henry had pulled the Line from practice and was relentlessly running the Indoor show. The Planets suite was slowly coming together. Each day, Bronwyn could see something that was a little bit better than they day before. She knew Henry was taking a risk with the program. The technical level of the show was intense and the sheer amount of drill was enough to do her head in, so there was plenty of room for error. However, if they managed to get it clean, then there would be no stopping the Forrest Hills drum line.

Without any of the previous year's pranks or distractions, the Homecoming game was as predictable as usual. The home team won and the Homecoming court looked amazing. Bronwyn and the boys had a killer time together. The redhead looked around and realized that despite the highs and lows of the season, she really was a part of the Line.

To: FHHSdmajor@FHHS.edu
From: karatechop@state.edu

Drew,

Your brother gave me your e-mail address. I've sat by long enough and I need to tell you I think you're making a colossal mistake taking Christina to Homecoming tomorrow. Take it from someone who knows, you don't want to look back and have regrets from your senior year.

B and I are going to have fun up here, far away from tacky backdrops and smelly corsages. I suggest you think about doing the same.

Lucy

After getting home from the Homecoming game, Bronwyn was far too excited for sleep. She began packing for the following day and night of fun with Lucy. Looking over her wardrobe, she sighed as she fingered a dress she had bought over the summer. No reason really, it was on sale and it was beautiful. It was the kind of dress you would wear to…

Nowhere.

Leaving the dress hanging in the closet, Bronwyn roughly zipped up her bag. The girls had tried to convince her to come and hang with them while they got ready for the big night, but she couldn't think of anything more depressing.

What did you think was going to happen?

Bronwyn pulled her knees up under her chin and tried to ignore the one or two tears that had somehow sneaked out.

That he was going to pick *me*.

You had the chance to go…

So that I could see them there together? I think not!

Buck up, drum line girls are made of tougher things. Anyway, you got what's important…

The Line. I just wish I could have it both ways.

There will be other boys.

I don't want other boys. I want Drew.

The next morning, Bronwyn waved goodbye to her parents as they dropped her off at the School of Music, assuring them that she would be fine. Her dad said, "Just call us when Lucy picks you up and if you need anything at all!"

"Yes, Dad."

"See you on Sunday – have fun and be safe."

Bronwyn walked into the building and signed in. Glancing over the list, she wasn't surprised to see a few names that she recognized from around the county.

Guess I'm not the only one who has better things to do today.

It was even more amusing, because many of the names on the list would be at the same place she was going to be in two weeks – the first Indoor competition of the season. Looking around the band room, Bronwyn was not at all surprised to see that she was the only girl in the group. She took a seat near the back, and the main clinician came out and started discussing the latest in drumming technology. After about an hour of speaking and a few demonstrations, the clinician addressed the group, "We've decided to pair you up with some of our music majors here at the school for a little more hands-on, personalized training. When you hear your name, I will call out the student you have been assigned to. He or she will raise their hand and you will work together for about an hour. "

Bronwyn listened until she heard her name called, "Flueger…Jeremiah."

Jeremiah? Jerm? Why does that name sound familiar?

Bronwyn caught the guy's eye and squinted, but couldn't remember where she recognized him from.

The announcer finished giving instructions, "Alright, we'll see everyone at around 11 back here in the band room."

Bronwyn walked up and introduced herself, "I'm Bronwyn."

"Jerm."

There was something oddly attractive about the guy in front of her. They walked down the hall to one of the practice rooms. Jerm asked, "Where do you go to school?"

"Forrest Hills."

"No shit. I used to go there."

"When did you graduate?"

"Let's see…three years ago."

"We missed each other by a year then."

Jerm had set up a practice stand, "Let's see what you got."

Bronwyn had no fear in her drumming, she peeled off the new snare solo from the Indoor show.

"Henry?"

Bronwyn nodded. There was an awkward moment between them. She sensed something was wrong with Jerm and asked, "What's up?"

"Oh, it's just weird to think about someone else on the Forrest Hills drum line. I mean, you'd like to think that the Line can't exist without you, but life goes on and people keep drumming."

What he was saying made sense in a weird way to Bronwyn, so she nodded. As they drummed and talked, the time went by quickly. Jerm was impressed with her new cadence, and had some things for her to work on. Finally, Jerm glanced up at the clock, "We'd better go."

Bronwyn smiled at the former Captain realizing that in a few years (hopefully!) she would join him in the long line of former Captains. As they walked back down the hall to the band room she said, "If you're not doing anything next weekend, you should come check out our show."

Jerm replied, "Yeah, I'll think about it. Keep working on your left hand sticking and maybe I'll see you around."

Chapter Nineteen
The Minor Fall, The Major Lift

After the clinic finished, as promised, Lucy and Pam were waiting for her outside the old building. The former bass drummer's face lit up in a smile as she wrapped her younger friend in a hug and asked, "How was it?"

"It was great. I learned a lot."

"Glad to hear it." With Pam trailing, Lucy began speaking very quickly, "Well, let's get started then. First, I thought we'd head back to my place so you can drop off your stuff, then maybe we'd get something to eat, or we could go downtown and go shopping – there's a cool store you've got to see."

"Anything sounds great." Bronwyn dug around in her jeans and fished out some money and handed it to Lucy, "My parents said they remember what it was like to be in school. So, this weekend is on them!"

"You have some cool parents, B."

"Yeah?"

"Definitely. Anyway, now that you're here, Pam and I are going to do our best to help you forget all about Forrest Hills and the craziness you left behind."

Already, Bronwyn felt better. She had had a morning doing what she loved most, and now she was going to have a complete weekend of freedom with her friend. Scooping the pug up, she said, "Thanks! So, will I get to meet Joe later?"

"He's working as a bar back these days, so I never know when he's going to turn up. Still, I think I convinced him into making us breakfast tomorrow morning. He does a great omelet."

Bronwyn was glad at least someone was having luck with an O'Malley male and replied, "Sounds yummy." She carefully put Pam back on the ground and said, "But, Lucy, I have to ask, are you sure you don't mind me coming up here? I mean, this is like your one three day weekend for the whole semester."

"Seriously, it's no big deal. I'm just coming off a big round of tests, and I didn't want to do anything else but chill out for three days. I wouldn't have invited you if I didn't want you here, okay?"

"Okay."

"Well, let's get to it then – I'm sure you worked up an appetite this morning."

A few hours later, Drew looked at himself in the mirror. In the reflection he saw himself, in a dark suit complete with aviator shades and polished black shoes. He looked again, squinting at his reflection. There was so much of this season he couldn't take back, so much of the year where he had waited and reacted instead of choosing to make the first move.

Coward.

What can I do?

Drew couldn't bear to think things through. He grabbed the flowers he had picked up for his date, jumped in the car and sped off.

Many hours and many, many calories later, Bronwyn and Lucy were in the middle of making root beer floats with Lucy's cute neighbors, Ryan and Matt. The high school sophomore had been shy at first, but being around Lucy and away from the drama of her life, Bronwyn happily settled into the spontaneity of college life. As they wished good night to the guys and returned to Lucy's apartment, the brunette rummaged around her DVD collection and shouted, "Aha! *10 Things I Hate About You*, just what I was looking for. You game?"

Bronwyn nodded and Lucy sprang up, "Popcorn first!"

"I couldn't possibly eat any more!"

Just then there was a knock at the door. Lucy looked at Bronwyn and shrugged, "It's probably my good for nothing neighbors wanting to borrow something. Let em' in."

Bronwyn opened the door saying, "I thought I told you we ran out of root beer…" The words died on her lips.

In front of her, dressed impeccably in a dark suit was none other than Drew, and he was holding a bouquet of beautiful stargazer lilies. Lucy called from the kitchen, "Who is it?"

Bronwyn couldn't speak. Drew smiled at her and answered, "It's Drew."

Bronwyn swore she could *hear* Lucy smile from the kitchen as her friend responded, "It's about damn time you showed up!"

Drew winked at a still speechless Bronwyn and said softly, "I think we need to talk." To Lucy, he called over Bronwyn's shoulder, "Can I borrow your house guest for a few minutes?"

The brunette poked her head around the corner and said, "Stargazers? My favorite!" She grabbed the flowers and shooing the younger pair outside, continued, "Borrow away."

Bronwyn could only stare in mute fascination as Drew took her hand and they began walking towards campus. The redhead considered the super weird day she had so far. Somehow, Drew showing up kind of fit in with everything. She still didn't trust her voice, so she was glad when Drew finally started talking, "I owe you an apology."

"I—"

"Let me finish. The night when everything happen, and you were at my car, and I totally ignored you, that was a really stupid move on my part and I'm sorry."

Bronwyn finally found her voice, and asked, "So, why Christina? Was that another 'stupid move?'"

Drew didn't say anything.

"I think I deserve an answer," Bronwyn pressed.

Drew slowly loosened his tie and finally replied, "I thought you were somehow involved with either, um, Ben or maybe Geoff."

Something about his completely erroneous ideas struck Bronwyn as funny, and she said, "Me? And Ben?! No way! Why didn't you just ask me about it?"

Drew was glad it was dark out, because his cheeks were suddenly very red. He raked a hand through his hair and answered, "I don't know. I really don't and then I started dating Christina and it just got all mixed up."

"Did you ever really like her?"

"Not like I liked…it wasn't ever the same as…"

Bronwyn understood what he was trying to communicate, but needed to actually hear him say the words, "So, what are you doing here?"

"Lucy kind of gave me the nudge I needed last night. I was getting ready to go and then, well, where else would I be?"

"I'm glad you came."

Drew's face lit up in a smile and he said, "So, I know I've been an ass most of the season, but there's a reason I'm here. Look, Bronwyn, can you forgive me?"

Bronwyn thought about what a funny pair they made at the moment, she in her jeans and t-shirt, Drew in his suit. She stopped and looked up at him. A cool breeze blew through the campus and she rubbed her hands on her arms, trying to warm up. Drew slowly took off his suit coat and put it on Bronwyn, tightening it around her shoulders. He kept his hands on her arms and slowly pulled her closer to his broad chest.

"Can you?"

Bronwyn was overcome with shyness and looked down at the ground.

"Please?" Drew's voice was almost a whisper and then his fingers were suddenly under her chin and slowly lifting her gaze up. He kissed her softly at first, then gave in to almost two months of pent up feelings. Bronwyn felt being herself carried away to a place where time seemed to stop and all that existed was Drew and his fabulous kisses.

"Eh-hem," a distinctively female voice said behind them sometime later.

Bronwyn flushed and tried to burrow into Drew's chest. He put his arms protectively around her.

"What's up, bro?"

Bronwyn slowly turned around and saw Lucy and some guy who could only be related to Drew walking towards her with Pam on the leash between them. Lucy grinned, "You guys were gone so long, I started to get worried. We'll see you back at my place in a few minutes?"

Bronwyn nodded. They watched Joe and Lucy walk away.

When the older couple was out of sight, Drew asked, "Am I forgiven?"

Bronwyn smiled and said, "You certainly are."

Miles away from the happy reunion, Christina Feldman looked at herself in the mirror and was very pleased with what she saw. She looked perfect. Her long mahogany hair was fastened in an elegant upsweep. Her nails were painted in a delicate French manicure. Her dress was a beautiful sky blue…all she was missing was her date. After months of crushing on him, she couldn't believe she was finally dating Drew. Her senior year was going exactly as planned.

She checked the clock again; Drew had said he would show up a little after 7PM. The appointed hour came and went and slowly dragged to eight. She had already left numerous calls and text messages on his phone, all of which had gone straight to voicemail. After an hour, she began receiving calls from her friends who were already at Homecoming wondering where she was. She lied smoothly, telling them they were having car trouble and would arrive at the dance shortly.

As eight pushed to nine, Christina impatiently phoned Drew's house, "Hello?"

Drew's mother, Anne, answered the phone, "Hello, O'Malley residence."

"Hi, Mrs. O'Malley, this is Christina."

"Oh, hello, dear, is something wrong with Drew?"

"I was hoping you could tell me."

"What do you mean? Isn't he with you?"

"He is most certainly not with me!"

"Well, that's strange, he left here a while ago…" Anne had privately wondered about her son's behavior as he left the house. Having two boys, she was pretty clued into their moods. Drew had been a little tense as he walked out the door.

"I hope nothing's happened to him."

Anne pondered a minute, believing that if something happened to either of her boys, she would probably be aware of it by now. She told the girl on the other end of the line, "Let me check with his brother. Should I call you back?"

"Just tell him I'll be at the dance."

And with that, Christina abruptly hung up the phone. Anne looked at the device, muttering something about 'young people these days' and quickly called her older son's cell phone number, "Joseph?"

When it came to their mother, both of the O'Malley boys usually paid attention. Joe answered immediately, "Hey, Ma. What's up?"

"Have you seen your brother?"

"Who wants to know?"

Anne paused before saying, "Drew's Homecoming date."

"He's, um, indisposed at the moment."

Anne sighed, but answered, "As long as he safe, that's what matters for now. Should I assume he will be spending the evening with you tonight and I will see you both tomorrow in time for dinner?"

"Yes, Ma."

"I love you, Joseph."

"I love you, too." Joe hung up the phone, and smiled politely at Lucy, "I'm going to kill my brother."

"What did he do?"

"Skipped out on his Homecoming date."

Lucy rolled her green eyes, "Will you boys never learn?"

As a response, Joe wrapped his arms around Lucy and said, "They were pretty cute together, weren't they?"

Lucy nodded, "I think she was worth whatever crap he's going to have to deal with in the next couple of weeks."

As Bronwyn and Drew walked back to Lucy's apartment, the sophomore snare started mentally freaking out. She knew he was supposed to be at Homecoming with Christina and had a sinking suspicion that Drew had not disclosed his current location to her. Furthermore, given what had taken place over the past half hour or more would definitely count as cheating. Not wanting to ruin the magic of the evening, Bronwyn decided to let things slide for now and worry about labels and more difficult conversations until tomorrow. Back at the apartment, there was talk of having the guys sleep over, but due to a lack of sleeping arrangements and a look of panic in Bronwyn's eyes, Lucy pushed the guys out around two in the morning, and said, "Can I assume Drew will be escorting Bronwyn home tomorrow?"

Drew smiled and answered, "I'll be back around 11."

Lucy's front door closed and as soon as Bronwyn heard Drew and Joe's voices trail off into the night, she picked up a bewildered Pam and screamed, "Aaaahhhh! That was the best night of my life!!"

"So, I take it things are good between you two?"

Bronwyn stopped dancing around the apartment, placed the dizzy dog on the ground, and said, "Yes. I mean, I just didn't think things were ever going to actually work out, but then, he just showed up, and…"

Lucy nudged her friend, "And what? Something like I saw earlier?"

Bronwyn's cheeks flamed red.

"So, what are you going to do about Christina?"

Bronwyn shrugged, "Not sure yet. We were having such a good time tonight that I didn't want to wreck things by bringing her up, y'know?"

"I'm sure he'll break things off with her."

"Yeah, I know it sounds bad, but I kind of hope so."

Lucy opened up a blanket and spread it over the couch, then commented, "Of course, that's if she doesn't break up with him first. Standing someone up the night of Homecoming is pretty much grounds for getting dumped. So maybe it will all work out."

Bronwyn yawned, suddenly exhausted from the long day, "After everything we've already been through this season, I'm sure we can handle her."

After a delicious breakfast prepared by Joe, Drew and Bronwyn were all smiles as they drove home the next day. Bronwyn leaned on Drew's shoulder and asked, "So, what happened last night?"

Drew knew she wasn't referring to *their* night together, but rather his botched Homecoming attempt, "Oh, I, um, didn't show up."

"That's what I was afraid of."

"I don't know what came over me. I looked in the mirror and then I just jumped in my car and started driving up here."

While Bronwyn was touched by the supremely romantic gesture, she was also freaking out a little about the wrath of Christina that would inevitably follow. In the light of day, she knew the Guard Captain was going to blame one person for Drew's disappearing act. She sighed and slid down in her seat, "She's going to kill me."

"Why you? *I'm* the one who stood her up."

Bronwyn's grey blue eyes were wide and she said, "You don't understand. In her world, I forced you to come up and be with me. She's going to flip."

"How about we don't tell her?" Drew asked, only half kidding.

Bronwyn shot him a look.

"Okay, so I know I need to break up with her. Maybe I just won't give her all of the explicit details."

"Can you do your best to convince her that I had nothing to do with this, please?"

"I still don't see why you're so worried, but yes, I'll try and mention it… or not mention you at all."

"That's all I'm asking for."

Too soon, they were pulling up to Bronwyn's house. Drew grabbed her hand and planted a kiss on her callused fingers, "See you tomorrow?"

"You want to take this thing public?" Bronwyn asked nervously, "Because I mean, you don't have to or anything, I'm really just happy to be—"

"Shhh. Yes, I want everyone in the Forrest Hills band to know that you are my girlfriend."

Bronwyn flushed, but managed to say shyly, "I'm glad to hear you say that."

She gathered up her bag and impulsively kissed Drew on the cheek, before sprinting out of the car, quickly saying hello to her parents and jumping on the phone to call an emergency meeting at the nearby Espresso Royale Café with Meredith and Megan.

Reminding himself he needed to do the right thing, Drew called Christina straight after leaving Bronwyn's house. Driving to the Guard member's house, he realized how guilty he looked, still in his rumpled suit from the night before.

Christina answered the door, and joined him on her front porch. She sat across from him and, toe tapping impatiently, asked, "Where were you?"

"Christina, I…"

"You couldn't even call?"

"I was a jerk. I know that."

"And?"

"And what?"

"Aren't you going to at least say you're sorry? That's the least you can do for your girlfriend!"

Drew pushed a rock on the ground with his foot, "Not exactly."

"Why the hell not?"

"I, um, well, that's part of the reason I didn't show up last night. I know this is going to sound bad, but, well, I think we should date other people."

Christina crossed her arms, and stated in a dark tone, "So, let me get this straight. You don't bother showing up for Homecoming, you have no excuse for it, you don't even bother to apologize and now **you** want to break up with **me**?"

"I—"

"Because let's get one thing straight, I am dumping **you**!"

Drew shrugged and said, "If that's what you want."

Christina, despite the tough exterior she was trying to convince Drew of, was slowly cracking. She continued, "It is! Your ass is dumped!"

Christina stood up, walked inside, slammed the door behind her, and desperately wished she felt more like she had come out on top of things.

Chapter Twenty

Crossing the Line

Settled in their favorite booth at the local coffee shop, Megan and Meredith looked over at Bronwyn, worried expressions on both of their faces. Megan was the first to venture a question, "So, emergency meeting, huh? Did something happen to Lucy?"

Bronwyn was attempting to keep a straight face, but couldn't keep up the charade. A large grin broke across her features and she said, "Not exactly."

Meredith asked, "Then what happened? You were only gone one night!"

"Drew came up to see me!"

Megan and Meredith sat back in the booth, clearly not expecting that answer from their friend. Bronwyn continued, "It was just, well, magical…"

Megan asked, "But what about Christina? Where exactly does she fit into this whole situation?"

"Umm, that's the part I need help with. Drew didn't exactly, um, inform her that he was going to, um, not going to go with Homecoming with her. He just kind of showed up on my doorstep. I mean, Lucy's doorstep."

"He what?!" Megan asked.

Bronwyn stirred massive quantities of sugar into her latte and said lamely, "It sounds just as bad as I think it does, doesn't it?"

Meredith said, "It certainly does. Do you feel like going on the offensive?"

"How do you mean?"

Meredith continued, "You could call her and explain you really had nothing to do with it."

"Do you think she would listen? Imagine if Ben had not shown up last night and was suddenly dating someone else, how would you feel if that person called you?"

Megan whistled slowly, "You are so dead."

Although she was terrified of what Christina would do when she found out, Bronwyn was flattered when Drew picked her up the next morning. Strapping herself in, she asked cautiously, "Did you talk to her?"

"Yup."

"Did you mention me?"

"No."

"How did she take it?"

"Not good."

"Should I be worried?"

"Maybe."

Bronwyn thought for a moment. It was probably better that Drew hadn't mentioned the specifics of why he had ditched his Homecoming date, but it was getting unbearable waiting for the other shoe to drop.

Maybe I should've called her, then at least it would've been out there already.

It's too late now, it's like Henry said, you've made your decision and now you just have to go with it, besides, what's the worst she can do?

Christina's sapphire eyes were glued on the band room door. She looked away for a moment and her eyes widened in surprise as she looked back to see a very happy Drew walking in, hand in hand with a radiant Bronwyn Flueger.

By Tuesday's practice, it was obvious to everyone in the Forrest Hills marching band that Bronwyn and Drew were a couple. The infamous "bet" which had stressed Bronwyn out so much, seemed like an eternity ago, and no one else seemed to remember the details anyway. And somehow, the drum major who had looked perfect with the beautiful Guard Captain, looked equally cute with the redheaded sophomore percussionist.

As Bronwyn walked down to the practice field, Geoff caught up with her. She looked down at her snare for a long moment and admitted, "I wanted to tell you..."

Geoff smiled companionably, "I won't hold it against you, but, as your friend, I have to ask, wasn't there some sort of bet taken against you earlier?"

"About that..."

"Yes?"

"Well, similar to the Hollaback scheme, I may or may not have had something to do with that whole situation."

"People don't give you enough credit, do they?"

"You have *no* idea."

"And here I thought you were just another pretty face."

Bronwyn blushed and replied, "After a season surrounded by guys, you would think I might have picked up a thing or two."

Drew joined the pair and asked, "What are you two talking about?"

"Nothing," came the automatic reply from both.

However nice it was to be someone's girlfriend, it was terrifying to be someone's worst enemy. As Bronwyn had predicted, Christina had not taken well to Drew's instant action to 'see other people.' Unfortunately, after showing up alone to Homecoming and the subsequent and obvious relationship between Drew and Bronwyn, the rumors surrounding the Guard Captain had not been kind.

"I heard she's been paying him this whole time…"

"I heard Bronwyn and Drew have been secretly dating since August…"

"I heard that Drew completely stood her up…"

With all of her concentration on learning the Indoor show, Bronwyn didn't have any extra energy to worry about waiting for the other shoe to drop. She could only hope Christina didn't find out the truth of where Drew had been on Homecoming evening until some time much later, and that maybe, just maybe, the Guard Captain would move on and find someone else to make her happy.

Unfortunately, luck was not on Bronwyn's side. Dana, who had heard from Tony about whose company Bronwyn had been in on Saturday night, told her Captain the bad news at practice. She finished by asking, "So, what are you going to do about it?"

Christina, momentarily distraught, fought back tears of rage and humiliation. Then, as a brilliant plan occurred to her, she asked the sophomore conversationally, "You don't really *like* Tony, do you?"

As much as she wanted to spend all available time with her new boyfriend, Bronwyn's budding romance with Drew was put on a temporary hiatus. At this moment, practicing and devoting all available energy to the Indoor show was more important. She had to be content to see him before school as the Line was practicing after school every day for the next two weeks and the majority of weekends as well.

At the Thursday practice before the first Indoor competition, as was now tradition, the rest of the band was invited to watch their percussionists' show. Bronwyn was so proud of the Line and intent on her performance that she didn't notice Christina and Dana watching with *way* more interest than two Guard girls should have regarding the drummers' drill.

After Friday's game, Drew drove Bronwyn home. She asked tentatively, "I thought Christina handled things very well this week, didn't you?"

Drew laughed, but said, "With the exception of the frosty stares and silent treatment I've been getting from her, I'd actually agree with you."

"Well, this may sound immature, but I really expected some sort of retribution and so far, so good. I have to give her props for acting like an adult."

Drew nodded and pulled into the driveway. He asked, "So, I'll see you tomorrow?"

"You really don't have to come up—"

"I want to support my girlfriend tomorrow," he interrupted.

Bronwyn still got a secret thrill when Drew called her his girlfriend. She replied, "Okay, I'll look for you after Prelims."

Drew grinned and leaned in for a good night kiss that took all thoughts of percussion and ex-girlfriends far away.

The following morning, Bronwyn tried to control her excitement for the Indoor competition – her first as a member of the Battery. There had been a large debate over what their uniforms would be this year. In the end, they had decided on Mars, and creatively filled in the large spectrum of the color red.

Bronwyn had personally opted for red patent leather pants that were a) totally awesome and b) she could only get away with wearing on the court. Her shirt was a black tank top with flames at the bottom. J.D. had splurged for the group and bought everyone on the snare line flame wristbands. The rest of the snares were literally in head to toe red and flames. Adam had found flame emblazoned Chuck Taylors online and ordered a pair for everyone (including Henry). With the addition of some dramatic make up and temporary hair color, they were an intense group.

The Line did not have as many individual competitors as the previous year, with only J.D. entering himself into the snare solo category. Bronwyn eagerly watched her Captain and the other competitors. She was planning on entering a solo she was working on next year and took mental notes about what worked and what did not. After the mandatory support of their Captain, the Forrest Hills drummers worked out their nerves and spent the afternoon working through parts of the show. Bronwyn was legitimately surprised everything had come together so smoothly. After such a disastrous season on the field, it had been a happy turn to have an Indoor show that clicked. After some tuning, and a tight warm up, the Line was pumped to go in and kick some serious ass.

"And now, under the direction of Henry Gough, Forrest Hills High School is prepared to present their show, The Planets, for competition. Drummers, are you ready?"

J.D. cracked off the familiar Mars refrain, and saluted with his sticks.

"You may begin."

The show started, moving seamlessly through selections from Holst's famous work. During the Pit feature, she looked into the audience and made eye contact with Drew, who, she was happy to see had made it up for the Prelims. He smiled at her and flashed a quick thumbs up.

Bronwyn concentrated on her part, and during a crossover move in the drill, dared another look up in the stands. She was shocked to see Christina practically sitting in Drew's lap, trying, it seemed, to plant a big kiss somewhere in the vicinity of her boyfriend's mouth. Bronwyn knew she had nothing to get jealous about; Drew was obviously struggling to get out of the embrace. However, like a car crash, she couldn't look away from the scene that was unfolding.

The day might have played out differently if that moment of particular drill didn't have the snares so close to the back court line. Without meaning to, Bronwyn stepped clearly out of bounds. It was so quick and she stepped back as soon as she realized what she had done. It was at that moment that she locked eyes with a judge.

What have I done...? Bronwyn's heart shuddered in her chest.

The rest of the show went smoothly – the best run through yet. As they came off the court, Bronwyn could see the looks of anticipation and excitement as the drummers walked off the court, obviously expecting high scores and a definite pass to the Finals later that evening. Bronwyn wanted to cry. There was no doubt in her mind she had stepped out of bounds. There was no doubt the judge had seen her do it. Were their scores high enough to still make it into the evening competition? As she dared one more glance at the stands, she saw a very smug grin on the face of Christina. Had the Guard member planned for this to happen?

J.D. clapped an arm around Bronwyn and hugged her close to his larger frame, "Great job out there, B! I can't wait for tonight! We're going to kick ass."

Bronwyn cringed and couldn't hold back her emotions any longer. Her bottom lip quivered, and she felt tears leaking out and not even pausing to take off her drum, she ran into a deserted women's bathroom. She didn't want to hear the results of the Prelims, knowing that she was the one solely responsible that her Line wouldn't be moving on to Finals. Even worse, the reason was one she could have controlled! She didn't drop a note or miss a step; she lost her concentration and walked right out of bounds. Bronwyn cried...for her seniors and her Line. Hearing someone behind her, she looked up and saw, of all people, Tony.

"Are you done yet?"

Bronwyn desperately wiped at her face and murmured, "Yes. Wh-what are you doing here?"

"I saw."

Bronwyn wasn't shocked. The drill had Tony far enough back from her that he could've seen her misstep, "Did you tell J.D.?"

"No. I knew it was coming."

Bronwyn's eyes widened she asked very slowly, "What do you mean, 'you knew?'"

"Dana asked me after practice on Tuesday about all the rules of Indoor. I thought she was just being a good girlfriend." He continued bitterly, "She saw how close the snares got to the edge of the court on Thursday."

"She was getting information for Christina?"

"Exactly. I didn't realize what was going to happen until we walked on the court and I saw Christina in the stands. By then it was too late."

Tony and Bronwyn sat in the empty women's bathroom. Bronwyn sighed, "It will be on all the tapes and the video. J.D. is going to kill me."

"There's always next week."

"But—" Bronwyn was still upset.

"Look, I'm breaking things off with Dana. I'm beginning to think she only dated me as some sort of weird way to get on the Line."

Bronwyn was surprised to hear actual regret in Tony's voice. Her section mate continued, "Let's talk to J.D."

"You'd help me out?"

"Sophomore snares have to stick together, don't they?"

Bronwyn gave her former enemy a half-smile.

After Bronwyn found a safe place for Stewie, the pair found their Captain in the stands. Tony was about to speak, but Bronwyn shook her head and said, "J.D., I have to talk to you."

"Right this very second?"

Bronwyn nodded. J.D., seeing Tony behind her and Bronwyn's tear stained face, said slowly, "Okay."

They walked out into the cool night, and stopped near the equipment truck. Bronwyn took a deep breath and admitted, "I stepped out of bounds."

"You did *what*?!"

Tony stepped in front of Bronwyn and said, "But it wasn't her fault."

"Let me get this straight, did someone *make* you step out of bounds?" J.D. sputtered.

Bronwyn was fully prepared to take the blame of the situation herself. She shook her head, "No."

Tony shook his head, "Yes."

Both heads turned to look at Tony. J.D. scowled, "What do you mean?"

Tony answered, "Bronwyn was set up. Christina distracted her. She knew exactly when Bronwyn was near the back line and she made her move then."

"I'm supposed to believe we won't be going to Finals all because of some Guard chick?"

"She was sitting on my boyfriend's lap, trying to suck his face off. I'm sorry that distracted me. I wasn't expecting to see it."

Suddenly, Drew came running around the corner, "Bronwyn!"

All three percussionists looked at the drum major. Drew didn't seem to care that J.D. and Tony were there and began apologizing, "You have to believe me! She came out of nowhere, she was like a vampire!"

Bronwyn smiled shyly, "I know, I saw the whole thing."

J.D. and Drew looked at each other. J.D. said, eyes narrowed, "I seem to recall you were going to have nothing to do with our Line, Drew."

Drew said proudly, "I'm not here as a drum major, J.D. I'm here as someone's boyfriend."

J.D. took a moment before he finally responded, "Thanks for coming out and supporting the Line."

"I wouldn't miss it for anything."

J.D. put his fingers on his temples as he looked back at the sophomores, "So, let me get this straight. Christina makes a move on your man, you get distracted, and take a step outside the line?"

Bronwyn nodded. Tony added, "But she knew when to make the move."

"How does some chick know about our drill? They only saw the show two days ago…"

Bronwyn sprang to Tony's rescue, "*He* was being used by Dana."

J.D. looked skeptical, "That's a lot of conspiracy just to get our Line knocked out of Finals."

Drew crossed his arms, "If you want someone to blame, I think you should blame me. I ditched Christina at Homecoming and instead of getting back at me, she chose to take out her aggression on Bronwyn instead. If I had just admitted my feelings for Bronwyn a month ago, then you would all be able to compete."

Suddenly, the awkward quartet was joined by the rest of the Line. Lance looked miserable as he announced, "We didn't make Finals."

Chapter Twenty-One

Battery Operated

Bronwyn looked around at the disappointed faces and felt even worse – without making the final competition, there was no chance at captions or section trophies. The redhead was expecting her Captain to make a big scene and point fingers strongly in her direction and that she would end up walking back to Forrest Hills. Somehow, inexplicably, and out of character, J.D. remained perfectly calm. He addressed the group, "That really sucks, but we'll have to wait and see what the tapes say on Monday."

Drew and Bronwyn shared an incredulous look, and then Bronwyn looked over at J.D., mouthing the words, 'thank you.'

Henry spoke up, "Let's all head back inside. We're going to want to watch the Lines that made Finals, so we can be ready for next week."

Drew and Bronwyn walked together slowly and Bronwyn leaned on Drew's shoulder. Wrapping a strong arm around her, he said, "I'm sorry."

"For what?"

"I really should've said something a month ago. I feel like you wouldn't be in this situation if I had just admitted that, I, um, that I liked you."

"That's okay. I'm just glad you didn't go to Homecoming with Christina. I'm not sure if I would've been able to get over that."

Suddenly, Bronwyn giggled. Drew looked down at her, "What's up?"

Bronwyn burst into uncontrollable laughter, "She was really going to suck your face off."

Drew exclaimed, "Hey now! That's not funny. You weren't on the other side of that!"

Reluctantly breaking contact with her boyfriend she said, "Well, I have to catch up with the rest of the Line. I'll see you on Monday?"

Drew gave her a lengthy kiss good night, ending it and murmuring in her hair, "It's not your fault. You did a great job tonight."

Bronwyn smiled and went in search of Henry, who she found inside at the concession stands. Dreading his response, she gathered what courage she had and calmly walked over to his side. Henry took a bite of his hot dog, chewed slowly, and said, "I saw."

Bronwyn was devastated all over again and apologized, "I'm so sorry."

Henry finished his food, swallowed, and replied, "Not so fast. I also saw what was going on in the stands."

"It's no excuse—"

"Bronwyn, please don't feel that way. It's *okay* for you to have a life outside of drumming. Seriously, I know being a percussionist is awesome, but you have to have balance in your life. I mean, you're only in high school and when you graduate you want to look back and have more than just memories of the Line."

"Still…"

"Believe me. Plus, we still have another week."

"But I—"

"Just say 'I'm sorry Henry, and it will never happen again.'"

"I'm sorry Henry and it will never happen again."

The tapes on Monday revealed exactly what Bronwyn was terrified they would.

"…watch it snare…watch it!" These words were followed by an audible sigh on the tape, and the judge continued, "Sorry, Forrest Hills drum line, but it looks like one of your percussionists stepped out of bounds. Per the rules of the competition, I'm going to have to deduct points."

The judge immediately went onto his next comment, but everyone in the Line looked at the snares. Bronwyn was slowly standing up, ready to take full responsibility for her actions, when J.D. looked sharply at her and she sat down. He paused the tape and addressed the percussionists, "Look, after we listen to the tapes, we're going to watch the video, and you're going to see who it was. Now, I know I wouldn't have said this earlier in the season, but it could've been any one of us and we're not going to win as a Line by putting all the blame on one person."

The drummers remained silent.

"We have one chance left, and I'd like to focus on that, rather than getting angry or punishing who it was. I know this person feels terrible about what happened, but it wasn't her fault." J.D. cringed at his pronoun slip.

With everyone's eyes instantly on her, Bronwyn stood up calmly and said, "Thanks J.D., I appreciate, well, I never thought I'd say this, but thanks for understanding."

J.D. looked at the ground before he looked up and said, "Look, I'm not too proud of how I handled myself early this season, Bronwyn. I thought if I was harder on you than anyone else, that, well I'm not sure. Anyway, the fact that you came to me and admitted your mistake says a lot about you. You could've tried to hide the fact or denied that it ever happened, but you didn't."

"It wouldn't prove anything," she admitted, and looked at the rest of the Line, "Seriously, this season is nothing like I thought it was going to be. I thought…well, it doesn't matter what I thought, but here we are and I can't undo my misstep. I can't give the seniors back their chance to win the competition, I can't let you all go to Finals. Believe me, if I could, I would. What I can do is promise that it won't happen again. I hope you can accept my apology."

The room was quiet again and Bronwyn wasn't sure what was going to happen next. She had visions of getting thrown out of the room, or a lifetime of physical punishments. Therefore, she was happily surprised when Tony said, "Like J.D. said, it could've happened to any of us, now, are we going to listen to the next tape, or what?"

No one argued, and in that moment, Bronwyn realized just how far she had come. J.D. nodded and moved to put the next judges' tape in the deck. As the group listened intently, Bronwyn couldn't believe everyone had so easily accepted her colossal mistake. She sat back in her chair and looked at the drummers. Ben caught her eye and smiled warmly. Feeling content, the snare drummer turned her attention back to the tapes, determined to make this weekend's show the best ever.

"Bronwyn?"
"Yes?"
"I want you to do something for me."
The redhead looked up at her boyfriend, and asked, "What?"
"Remember how you still owe me a favor?" He teased.
She wondered if he had remembered the promise she had made to him at band camp, and nodded in response.

"As much as I want to take care of things with Christina on your behalf, I think this is something you need to do. You can't just let her or Dana get away with things. You need to confront her."

"Yeah, but remember last year? I don't want to do anything that puts the Line, or me, in danger of not competing this weekend."

They walked silently together down to the practice field, each trying to think of a way around Mr. Izzo. A welcome distraction came as Bronwyn looked up at the band director podium and glimpsed a familiar brown ponytail. She said to Drew, "Don't worry, I got this."

"Okay, well, just know that I'll be around if you need me."

"Thanks!" The snare drummer zipped up her track jacket and caught Lucy's attention, waving her sticks wildly. In response, Lucy smiled and came over to meet her friend. They hugged awkwardly over Bronwyn's snare and Lucy said, "Sorry. I heard about Saturday. I was going to try and surprise you..."

"Here's the thing – you know what they did, and I can't let it slide. I want to tell them off in front of everyone, but I can't do that if Mr. Izzo is watching. Can you help distract him and give me a few minutes alone with those girls?"

"Say no more," Lucy's eyes narrowed, "Consider it done."

Bronwyn ran through the halftime show, but in spirit only. She was too busy trying to go over what she wanted to say to her two favorite Guard girls. The redhead kept an eye on Lucy, waiting for the right moment to make her move. The time finally came and Bronwyn cracked her knuckles and slowly put her drum down. She walked over to where the Guard had stopped on the last set, and said loudly, "Christina. Dana. I want to talk to you. Now."

Between all the rumors and highs and lows of the season, the members of the marching band were well aware of the friction between the Guard and The Girl on the Battery. Those who were within earshot, hovered closely, waiting to see what the outcome would be. Christina crossed her arms and turned around, her back towards Bronwyn. She looked at Dana and said in a bored tone, "Did you hear anything?"

Dana shook her head and followed her Captain's lead, "No."

"You crossed the line," Bronwyn challenged.

Christina's eyes narrowed and she spun around, exploding, "Are you sure it wasn't *you* who crossed the line? You *knew* Drew was taking me to Homecoming!"

"I didn't ask him to come and see me instead! He did that on his own!"

"Like I'm supposed to believe you? This coming from the girl who, well, I think given your reputation we all know why Drew likes you. I'm sure he'll get bored with that eventually and come back to me."

Bronwyn felt tears of anger and embarrassment pricking the back of her eyes and willed them away. She turned her attention to her classmate and said, "That's another thing I've been meaning to address, Dana."

Dana crossed her arms as Bronwyn continued, "I really don't appreciate the crap you've been spreading about me."

"Whatever."

Although Bronwyn had wanted to keep this between the three of them, Megan and Meredith had joined the trio, and like true friends, they weren't about to hold anything back. Megan exclaimed angrily, "Whatever?! Whatever!

You made up some pretty disgusting stuff, all because of some grudge that you didn't make the Line? Way to support Team Girl, Dana. Bronwyn is part of a six person section – all of whom helped decide that you weren't good enough to be a part of it."

Meredith added, "From what I heard, you couldn't even dream of making the Line."

Bronwyn smiled at her friends, glad for their support. She didn't even realize that Tony and a number of the other members of the Line had joined them. Tony said bitterly, "By the way, who is so desperate, pathetic, and immature they have to use people to wreck the lives of not just one person, but an entire section?"

Christina tried to speak, "I—"

J.D. added, "You'd better not plan on showing up this Saturday, Christina. From one Captain to another, I really don't appreciate what you did last weekend."

The two girls stared in shocked disbelief at the faces around them.

Drew, as drum major, had wanted to remain impartial, but this far in the season he really had nothing to lose. He joined the group and asked, "What did you think would happen on Saturday? Did you think no one would find out? Did you think I would come back to you? I'm really sorry for the way things worked out between us and if I could take them back, I would…all the way back. It's always been Bronwyn."

To accentuate his point, Drew walked up to Bronwyn and took her hand, which she was very grateful for. Drew's actions appeared to be just too much for Christina to handle. She began to cry, which Bronwyn was partially saddened to see. She hadn't really wanted to make someone that upset…

Well, maybe just a little bit. Remember how she kept you out of Finals?

Bronwyn said softly, "I'm sorry, Christina, but if you ever so much as look at *my* boyfriend or attempt to do something underhanded to corrupt me or my Line again, well, look who you're really dealing with."

Christina looked up and saw a number of people, all glaring coldly at her, and walked silently towards the school. Satisfied, Bronwyn finished, "And Dana? If you're still interested, let's just say you're going to have work really hard to get a place on the Forrest Hills drum line. If you hadn't heard already, we're one Line, one sound, and we don't like *anyone* who jeopardizes that."

Bronwyn didn't even both turning around to gauge reactions as she collected Stewie and went up to the blacktop where the Line was gathering for the Indoor run-throughs. As much as she was glad for her friends' support, she didn't really have the desire to be around anyone at the moment. Kicking the ground angrily, she didn't feel this was her proudest moment.

Watching Bronwyn's distracted look as she walked, Lucy was able to sneak up on the sophomore. She linked arms with her friend, "You did the right thing."

"I'm not so sure."

"Look – you put those girls in their place. If you weren't proud of yourself, then at least be proud of your own personal support team."

"You saw them?"

"Let's see, in one afternoon you've cemented your acceptance with the Line, stood up for yourself, claimed a boyfriend, and quite probably ensured your future as the Captain. You are a true leader."

"You think?"

"I know. Listen, no one ever said it was easy to be a girl and be a drummer. There's always going to be people on the outside, who don't know all the facts of what's actually going on. There's always going to be people who think one thing or another, but you learned a valuable lesson out of all of this."

"I did?"

"Be true to yourself. The rest will follow. I mean, are you going to look back at this season and have any regrets?"

Bronwyn brightened, "No. Not really, I guess, overall, it all worked out."

"Would you have rather had J.D. or Drew fight for you?"

"No – you and Drew were right, this was my fight."

"Then go get em' tiger, I can't wait to see this show."

Bronwyn joined the rest of the Line in a much better mood. After running through the show a number of times and fine tuning the most minute details, practice was over. Lucy called over to Bronwyn, "Great job out there. You want to join us at Waffle House?"

"Nah," Bronwyn said, and Drew walked up beside her, "Thanks for everything Lucy."

"No worries." She looked at her phone and said, "Well, I'd better get going so I can get my old seat. Take care, you two."

Drew called after her, "Say hi to my brother for me!"

"You got it!"

A few days later, on a clear Saturday afternoon in November, the Preliminary competition went better than anyone could hope for. The Forrest Hills drum line was not surprised to hear that they were going into the Finals in first place. During warm-ups for Finals, Bronwyn stared out in the crowd that had gathered to watch the Line and was surprised to recognize a familiar face looking back at her.

Jerm…?

She watched Henry and the former Captain talking and it looked like they were involved in more than just casual conversation. After Henry was satisfied with the warm up, tuning, and final run through of the show, the Line was ready to go in and compete for the first place trophy. Jerm walked alongside the drummers. Bronwyn smiled as he fell into step next to her.

"Looks like you took my advice," she commented.

"Looks like you took mine."

"So, what were you and Henry talking about?"

"Well, don't start any rumors, but I think Henry's time with the Line might be coming to a close."

With her junior and senior years ahead of her, Bronwyn definitely did not want to hear that information. Seeing the upset look on the sophomore's face, Jerm continued, "And since I'm a music major…well, it might be a good fit for me to come and take over. Or, at least to help out next season. I mean, Henry's been with this Line for a really long time, maybe it's time for him to move on."

"What about your college Line?"

"As fun at it is, it might be a different challenge to write a show. Plus, another guy I know might be returning to help his Line. If he goes back, I'm going to have to make sure my Line beats his."

Henry signaled for Bronwyn to join the rest of the snares. She called over her shoulder, "So, see you next year, I guess?"

"Something like that. Good luck out there."

As much as Bronwyn might have been distracted by the former Captain and what he'd told her, as soon as she entered the gym, she was all business. She was completely committed to her part and the next ten minutes. The announcer asked his familiar question, "Forrest Hills High School drum line, are you ready to take the court for competition?"

J.D. beat out the familiar refrain and with quiet 'duts' the show began. As she wound her way through the intricate drill patterns, Bronwyn realized she enjoyed the previous season's show, but there was something even better about being part of the snare line and Battery this year. After the final notes echoed off the gym walls, Bronwyn and the rest of the Line hurried off the court to thunderous applause. She rushed out to the truck and took off Stewie, placing the instrument carefully in its case. Wanting to simultaneously take a much needed trip to the bathroom, find Drew, and get a good seat for the final scores, Bronwyn found herself pausing in the early winter air. Somewhere between August and here, her season had turned out exactly how she wanted it to be. The highs and lows came together for something she would always remember.

"What are you doing out here? Don't you want to see how it goes?"

Bronwyn turned around and saw Drew's breath frosting in the air. She answered confidently, "I already know how it will end."

"How's that?"

She walked up and laced her fingers in his, "A happy ending."

Some time later, after saying a warm goodbye to Drew and promising to meet him at Forrest Hills, Bronwyn made her way to the buses and caught up with the rest of her rambunctious section. Tony exclaimed, "Hey, B! Got a seat right here."

The redhead shrugged and slid in next to her classmate.

"Where were you?"

"Someone had to look after the equipment."

Tony seemed too excited to really press for further details. He asked, "Guess what? We won!"

Bronwyn smiled and replied, "I know. I didn't have to be there to know that. We're the Forrest Hills drum line, after all."

"Yeah, but did you know about this?" He proudly held up the Best Snare trophy and said, "You ready to get our initials on this thing?"

Bronwyn nodded and pulled out her pink Swiss army knife, commenting, "I earned it, didn't I?"

Fin.
27.05.09
Dubai, UAE

Acknowledgements

So, as always, a gynormous thank you to the fans, readers, and friends who continue to motivate and inspire me.

The *Keeping in Line* you've just finished reading wouldn't have been half as awesome if not for the fabulous Joanne Hill. She really pushed it to the next level and for that I am forever grateful.

Finally, as basically another thank-you-for-being-awesome, I'd like to include an additional couple of short stories and small character development pieces for you to read. As you may have guessed – I really like my characters! However, it's sometimes fun to mix things up and write projects other than those which are novel length. Some fall in the category of 'drabbles,' which are basically 100 words about a particular topic. Another set of writing exercises is my quotes project, which are short scenes prompted by recognizable lines from different films and movies. Having read the other books in my series will be helpful, but not necessary, as most of these kind of stand alone. They are all pretty much self explanatory (I've given you a reference for the timing and which character it refers to if too vague), and hope you enjoy!

"What we do in life echoes in eternity."

Freshman Lucy Karate was so nervous, her teeth were literally clattering. It was the worst case of nerves she could ever remember. It was her first Indoor competition, minutes before they would take the court for Prelims. The Line had rehearsed enough that she knew her hands would be able to go through the motions, but was afraid of what her mind would do.

Rush the tempo…

Play during a rest…

Strike the wrong notes…

They were in the staging area, closely clumped together in the vaguely damp hallway near the gym. Lucy's trembling hands were on one side of the marimba, but she couldn't stop them from shaking. The Forrest Hills percussionists listened to the muffled beats and notes on the other side of the wall. South Washington was playing, and they wanted to hear their rivals.

Lucy, on the other hand, only wanted not to throw up.

"Nervous?" Cameron asked.

Now I am…

"Ummm…" Lucy was incapable of forming an actual word, especially this close to her season long crush.

"You'll be fine."

"Will I?"

"Just remember, what we do in life echoes in eternity."

She blinked a moment and replied, "And that's supposed to make me feel better?"

His answer was the whispered, "No, it's supposed to make you remember you are a member of the Forrest Hills drum line."

The applause thundered on the other side of the wall. South Washington had finished and it was their turn to play. Calmness set over Lucy, and she finally understood what all the attitude was about. Confidence replaced her nerves and she smiled at the upperclassmen.

"I am."

Mistletoe

Fourteen-year-old Forrest Hills freshman Lucy Karate paused at the door to the giant mansion in front of her, feeling like a complete and total loser. Her parents (with her dorky younger brother in tow) had just dropped her off at her first official high school party and she was pretty sure everyone inside had seen her "grand entrance." She contemplated turning around and getting right back in the car. However, it was too late as her family was already on their way to tour the holiday lights display in the upscale neighborhood. Lucy had a sinking suspicion it was so that they could be close by "in case anything happened."

Getting her Mom to agree to let her go to a party where there were going to be upperclassmen (emphasis on *men*) had been an uphill battle, but there was no way she was going to miss out on the fun – especially when her best friends Gina and Mandy were eagerly awaiting a full report on the festivities. She had briefly debated smuggling her pals in for confidence, but if there was once thing she had learned this season, it was that she was definitely becoming a stronger, more assertive individual. Besides, the drum line Christmas party was legendary and the only way of being invited was if you were a member of the Line, dating one of its members, or were an alumni home from college. The local percussion teacher (and father of three prominent Forrest Hills percussion alumni – two Captains no less), Mr. DiBonaventura, was a very wealthy man and loved entertaining. This party was a way to show his young drummers how much he appreciated them and how pleased he was of another award winning season.

Lucy felt proud of trophies she had helped win as part of the Pit. The season had been long and demanding, but worth every second. Still standing at the front door under the twinkling white lights, Lucy found herself wondering if she had a chance of making the Battery during auditions in the spring.

What a difference a semester makes…

A year ago, if asked what a 'battery' was, she probably would've thought about the device that charged things, now…she could only think of drums… and the boys that played them. Lucy looked down and questioned again if she had chosen the right thing to wear. Because this party was such a big deal (Mr. DiBonaventura's house was in the only gated community in the school district), Lucy's mom had taken her shopping for a real dress. After looking in practically every store in the mall, Lucy had lucked out and found a beautiful dress. It was a gorgeous silver halter dress that made her feel amazing – and was also on sale! The satin felt delicious on her skin, and with the combined efforts of her best friends, she knew her elegant upsweep was not going anywhere.

Except inside…

Give me a minute!

Uh, hello? Baby, it's cold outside!

Part of her still wanted to run home, throw on some old jeans and a hoodie, but in the end she was glad she chose the dress and to actually come to the party. It was all part of her goal to break out of her "shy Pit girl" persona and start to get some recognition in the section. What better place to start than the Christmas party? Currently, she had too many crushes to count, the top of her fantasy boyfriend list being none other than Cameron MacKenzie, snare hottie. Best of all, he was an upperclassman…not an annoying sophomore, like know-it-all first bass drummer, Spence. Lucy could count on one hand the times she had conversed alone with the flirtatious junior. Furthermore, the latest gossip was that Cameron was single! He had been attached to the pretty blonde Ellen from the Dance Line all season, but apparently something had happened and Lucy could only hope the rumors were true. Suddenly, she realized someone was behind her.

A masculine voice whispered in her ear, "You know, you might not believe it, but there's actually a party is inside. We don't force the freshman to stay outside."

Lucy looked up and gasped, Cameron was standing right next to her, looking dapper in a dark suit. The young front line member had to remind herself to breathe.

"Oh yeah?" Lucy finally responded and then wondered why Cameron seemed content to stand in the freezing cold with her.

Not that I'm complaining…

She closed her eyes and hoped that her cheeks were rosy and that her mascara hadn't clumped. From under her eyelashes, she realized that his usual electric blue gaze seemed not as intense as usual.

You could always ask him about it…

What's he going to do, spill his heart to some lame freshman he doesn't even know?

You'll never know until you ask.

"Is everything okay?" Lucy questioned, her breath making little white puffs in the cold December air.

Cameron rubbed his hands together for warmth and pasted a smile on his face. In what Lucy considered a very phony voice he replied, "Sure, fine. Why shouldn't I be?"

The freshman didn't really have a good answer to his question, so she shrugged her shoulders. The moment on the front porch, whether real or imagined, was broken. Cameron continued awkwardly, "Here, let me get the door for you."

"Thanks," Lucy tried to keep the disappointment out of her voice.

Hey now – six times you've talked! It's a Christmas miracle!

As soon as the pair entered the house, someone asked to take her coat and she watched helplessly as Cameron disappeared into the kitchen. Lucy sighed, but went off to find Molly, kind of second guessing why she hadn't volunteered to ride with the other Pit girl in the first place.

The freshman drummer was pleasantly surprised as the evening went by quickly and was embarrassed that it seemed she had to leave before anyone else. Carefully timing her exit, Lucy went over to retrieve her coat, hoping that no one would notice that her curfew was before anyone else's and that her parents were going to pick her up.

Come on Mom and Dad, why did we say eleven? No one else has to leave now!

With a final sigh, she buttoned up her jacket and realized she slightly disappointed with the way the evening had turned out. Sure, she had flirted and laughed and all the things you were supposed to do at a party, but there was something missing.

Hearing some of her classmates approaching and still obviously having a good time, Lucy quickly ducked into the deserted formal dining room. Wanting to stay warm, she was planning to wait until the last minute to run out and make a quick getaway when he parents pulled up.

"You leaving?" A familiar voice asked, causing her to turn around.

Lucy looked to see Cameron's muscular figure leaning on the doorframe. Trying not to stare, she quickly averted her gaze and happened to see that he was standing under some very strategically placed mistletoe.

Oh...my...gosh – did he just see me check him out **and** *look at the mistletoe?*

Lucy risked a glance in his direction – Cameron looked up and locked eyes with her, a slow grin stretching across his face.

"That's the first time you've really smiled tonight," Lucy blurted out.

From across the room, Cameron cocked his head at her, "How do you know?"

"Umm...I don't. Sorry, just ignore me." Lucy was glad it was dark in the room, because her cheeks definitely flushed.

"You might be right."

Lucy's heartbeat sped up as Cameron came into the room and stood across the elegantly set table from her. She willed her parents to be late, and looked outside. Her heart soared when she didn't see headlights. Deciding that the role of "sympathetic ear" might be her best option to continue conversation with her season long crush, Lucy asked warily, "*Are* you okay?"

Cameron responded in a distant voice, "Yeah."

"I don't believe you," she challenged.

"Really, Lucy?"

"Yes," she answered honestly.

Cameron traced a plate on the table. Not making eye contact, he asked, "Why don't you think I'm okay?"

Lucy gulped. Freshman boys she knew (or at least thought she knew) how to handle, but this was the first time she had ever been really alone with someone she was interested in. Unable to come up with anything, she finally found her voice and murmured, "I would say it's because of your recent breakup..."

Cameron didn't answer for a moment, instead taking time to walk further around the table, picking up a frame with Michael, last year's Captain, in his graduation robes. Setting it down carefully, he said, "How do you know that I'm not still dating her?"

"You would've brought her tonight," Lucy said mater-of-factly.

"Would I?"

"You would." Lucy had no doubt, because who wouldn't bring Ellen? She was gorgeous and lots of fun to be around.

I might as well keep on screwing things up...let's see, I've already called him unhappy, why shouldn't I throw 'wrong' into the mix for fun?

Lost in her thoughts, Lucy looked up and realized Cameron was suddenly very near. Not really answering her statement, he asked, "What do you want for Christmas, Lucy?"

Lucy wasn't about to tell him that all of the sudden something that you couldn't buy in stores had shot up to the top of the list – something that involved a small piece of shrubbery that was about five feet away. She shifted nervously and replied, "To make the Battery next year."

"That's all?"

Lucy was uncomfortable this close to her crush, so she moved towards the door, and said unconvincingly, "Yup."

"I don't believe you." He threw her own words back at her.

Lucy paused, and realized that *she* was now standing under the mistletoe.

"Do you believe in tradition?"

Lucy thought it was a weird time to bring up the drum line, but if it changed the subject away from something that didn't make her blush, then she would take it.

"Sure..."

Instead of responding, Cameron moved in so they were both standing in the crowded space of the doorway. In a good way, Lucy couldn't breathe, she looked down.

"Lucy…" A voice whispered very close to her face.

Lucy looked up and realized there were only inches separating she and Cameron MacKenzie. His eyes were twinkling and this close to him she noticed a light sprinkling of freckles across his nose.

"Now, are you sure there's nothing you'd like to ask Santa for?"

Lucy gulped; the tone in his voice alone was enough to make her melt.

All I want for Christmas is a perfect first kiss…

With her heart pounding in her chest, Lucy could only summon the courage to look up to where the mistletoe was hanging. The gesture was enough for the junior. As soon as Cameron's callused hand cupped her cheek, Lucy closed her eyes. With her heart pounding, the freshman thought time stopped as his soft lips met hers. Not wanting the moment to end, she put her arms around his neck, and responding to his tongue on her lips, did what came naturally – opening her mouth and deepening the kiss. As Cameron brought her in close, Lucy lost herself in the sensations of the embrace…until headlights flared in the room.

Breathlessly, Lucy stopped the kiss, but leaned in until she was forehead to forehead with Cameron. In a highly disappointed tone, she whispered, "I have to go."

Cameron murmured, "I know."

Lucy shyly smiled as she walked away and said, "Merry Christmas, Cameron."

"Goodbye, Lucy."

Something in his voice made her stop. She was going to ask, but her Dad honked the horn and she walked out into the cold night, trying to believe what had just happened wasn't a dream.

It really was the best Christmas Lucy could ever remember. On the morning of December 25th, she was having a wonderful dream about Cameron's perfect kiss, and turned over happily. As Cameron's kisses grew sloppier, Lucy's green eyes opened and she was ecstatic to see a small Pug puppy on her chest.

Lucy's squeals were heard throughout the house, "Thanks Mom and Dad! She's perfect!!!"

A few hours later, after all the presents had been opened, Lucy got on her computer to send out holiday wishes to everyone. Opening Facebook, she immediately zeroed in on Cameron's name and her eyes squinted in concern when she saw he had posted a note entitled, "Goodbye."

Holding her breath, Lucy was shocked to see the following note:

Hey dudes and dudettes,

My Dad got transferred and we're moving out of state. I enjoyed all of my seasons with the Forrest Hills drum line and am proud of every note I got to play with you guys. Best of luck to everyone in the future. I'll give y'all my contact info when we get settled.

Keep on rocking!

Cameron...

Death *(during **A Fine Line's** band camp, Tom's point of view, 100 words)*

"Yeah dude, it's dead."

"Aww...and I thought I was going to be first."

The tenor Lieutenant grinned at his section, got out his trusty drum key, and began unscrewing his largest drumhead – which was completely busted. After affixing the new one (which looked weird next to the other broken-in heads), he asked, "You know there's a tradition, right?"

"What's that?"

"It's like Frisbee and discus together. Whoever can chuck the broken head the furthest – wins!"

That's how Henry found his tenor section. Instead of memorizing the closer, they had taken a few moments to be high school boys.

Tie

"Lucy?"

The brunette in question turned, a faint blush creeping onto her cheeks. No matter how many times she heard it, the green eyed girl always got a small rush hearing her (what she regarded as boring and utterly normal) name spoken in the deliciously polite upper crust British tones of her boyfriend, Wes Mallinson.

"Yes?" Lucy responded, a small smile playing on her lips.

"A little bloody help here?"

Smiling, his girlfriend asked playfully, "How did you manage to get to the school in this state?"

Wes rumpled his wet from the shower hair in an entirely familiar gesture, and answered, "Umm, I don't know?"

Confidently, Lucy moved over and began retying the silk tie that was currently askew around Wes' dress shirt. Confused, the football player looked down at Lucy's nimble hands – her bass mallet calluses long gone – tie a perfect single Windsor. Wes gazed down lovingly at Lucy's face while she concentrated on the task at hand. Once the gray silk was securely in place, Wes asked, "Do I want to know how you know to do that so well?"

Lucy Elizabeth Karate really hadn't thought she would get emotional at her graduation, after all, she had had her entire senior year to prepare for it. However, the simple question triggered some undeniable fact. Being one of the sole drum line girls of the Forrest Hills HS marching band, it had always been *her* responsibility during concert season to make sure that her boys had their formal wear on appropriately. Now…abruptly, those days were gone. She wouldn't be tying anyone else's ties. Wouldn't be learning a new show. Wouldn't have lame inside jokes. *Who would make sure…?* A finger under her cheek interrupted her thoughts.

"What's the matter?" asked a concerned Wes.

Lucy quickly wiped away the two tears that had formed and pasted a smile on her features, "Nothing – let's go get our diplomas."

Irregular Orbit *(early in the season, **Keeping in Line**, 100 words)*

Bronwyn had to admit, marching was different than she expected it to be. Take for example, today's practice.

Henry shook his head, "Guys – I don't need to tell you that was horrible. Start again!"

The Battery grumbled as they reset the opening to the drum solo. Their Instructor clicked off counts on his drum sticks. This version wasn't as bad, although Bronwyn hadn't been quick enough and ended up just missing getting Tony's bass drum in her back.

"I told you – it's supposed to be an irregular orbit!"

J.D. asked, on everyone's behalf, "What does *that* look like?!"

Luck *(Bronwyn POV,* ***Keeping in Line,*** *100 words)*

Although everything had abruptly changed in the past two weeks (for the best!), I still felt I needed something to ensure my good luck. Looking around the percussion room as we packed up our equipment for the competition the next day, I looked on the percussion room wall. There was a busted shelf that held relics and trophies from previous Lines – plenty to be proud about, enough to find inspiration from. Tucked away, I unearthed a scratched up, spray painted, gold mallet. Attached to it – a note:

From the Front Line...

This mallet has magical properties – good luck!

Colors *(100 words)*

There were many significant colors that made up the Forrest Hills HS marching band.

The crisp kelly green of the uniform coats, so similar to the field on which they marched.

The solid black uniform pants, with matching dark berets and Shakos, and most recently the drumheads of the same color.

Shining silver, on the rims, on the keys, on the buttons, on the braids of the leadership who wore them proudly.

And finally, stark white – to match the hash marks and yard lines on the field, found in proud stripes on their uniforms, and the spats on their feet.

Boundaries *(circa **Keeping in Line**, 100 words)*

   bassgirl17: So, you're seriously not going to tell me?

   Cartwright213: No. As I've told you on numerous occasions, knowing who the other one was would *totally* defeat the purpose of our whole relationship. Things change when you know who you're talking to. What if I was really some old dude?

   bassgirl17: Then I'd still want to know.

   Cartwright213: Tough luck, kiddo.

   bassgirl17: …

   Cartwright213: I'm not budging.

   bassgirl17: Can we make a pact, that like, if we're still talking in 5 years or whatever, then we'll trade names?

   Cartwright213: Maybe we could…

   bassgirl17: I guess I can live with that.

Eternity *(100 words)*

Of all the band buses to break down, it was the drum line bus that did. While they waved goodbye to the others, the long wait set in for the magic part that was needed.

Lucy, who had already finished her homework, and didn't feel like helping Tom start his, laid down on the warm grass and idly wondered what it would be like to be stuck forever at a rest stop with the drum line.

Hearing the familiar sound of drum sticks on a practice pad, a random burp, and Molly's laughter, she decided it wouldn't be so bad.